THE LITTLE STONE ANGEL

ELLA CORNISH

This is a work of fiction. Any names or characters, businesses or places, events or incidents, are fictitious. Any resemblance to actual persons, living or dead, or actual events is purely coincidental.

Copyright © 2022 by Ella Cornish

All rights reserved.

No part of this book may be reproduced in any form or by any electronic or mechanical means, including information storage and retrieval systems, without written permission from the author, except for the use of brief quotations in a book review.

Email: ellacornishauthor@gmail.com

CHAPTER 1

*W*avering moonlight ignited the stone angel, casting an eerie halo about his crown. Masoned curls, hallowed eyes, outstretched finger, promising paradise just beyond his reach. Behind him, a white-washed church loomed forebodingly quiet, accenting the gleam of the statue in its foreground.

Jessica gawked, transfixed. She was sure she had never seen a sculpture quite this large and certainly not so close. She was eager to put her filthy fingers upon it, if only for a moment before Gareth took note of her waywardness. Her guardian did not understand Jessica's fascination with the angels, nor did he care for distractions. If he were to notice her straying from the task at hand, he would undoubtedly deliver swift justice and keep a steady eye upon her henceforth, ensuring that she would never again touch the stone faces she loved so much.

Yet the threat of Gareth's wrath did not sway the girl, the urge to feel the smooth marble betwixt her fingers unbearable. This angel called to her, summoning her forward with his hollow stare.

Toes pressing through the holes of her decrepit footwear, she rushed forward, crystalline eyes luminous in the midnight cemetery. She did not notice the sting of fresh cuts on her feet nor the flip-flap of worn leather slapping through the mud as she bustled forward. Jessica was grateful to have shoes at all, worn as they were. Erin had been forced to go barefooted after losing a boot in the Scotsman's courtyard on a jaunt earlier that week. Gareth refused to replace them, citing Erin's ungratefulness as reason but Jessica was sure he would change his mind soon. Erin was his favourite, after all.

The statue was almost within reach, Jessica stretching her own bony fingers to touch the idol as she neared. Had she minded her path, she would have foreseen the open grave before she was upon it—and ultimately in it. Her left foot tripped over an exposed root, the right following suit, plunging her downward, to Hell.

Scabbed knees accepted the brunt of her landing, the hem of her holed frock twisting over her legs and Jessica gasped, properly startled by her spill. After several silent seconds, she gleaned she was uninjured but that did little to placate her racing heart. Dark holes meant for corpses were no place for a girl of nine, even ones who pretended to be as fearless as Jessica, the girl with no surname.

But Jessica knew she was far from courageous, despite the face she put on for her urchin siblings and Gareth. Fear perpetually clung to her emaciated frame, thinly veiled and prepared to rear its ugly head at a moment's notice.

She tipped her tangled mop of dark hair back helplessly, searching upward for a means out. Once, her messy tresses

Jake stepped protectively closer to the smaller girl, his gangly body shadowing hers but disappeared against the backdrop of Gareth. At fifteen, he was the eldest of the urchin siblings, only by months in front of Erin, but years of living in harsh conditions made him appear much younger.

"Leave her be," Jake muttered, averting his eyes from Gareth's intense stare. He instead fixed his attention on Jessica. "Are ye 'urt?"

"It would serve her right if she were!" Gareth barked, face puckering more before Jessica could manage to shake her head.

"It wouldn't 'elp us none," Jake fired back. "We're already down a boy, right?"

Erin sighed and nodded in agreement.

"None of this would have happened if Liam were here," she mumbled sullenly. "He was like a cat in the dark."

Briefly, the children exchanged glances, the memory of their companion rushing pangs of longing through Jessica. Their exploits had been much weaker in Liam's absence.

Liam 'as found a "beautiful life," just as Gareth promised him. We mustn't fault him for that.

"Enough chatter!" Gareth thundered, sensing that he had lost their focus. "Off with the lot of you! Do what you've come to do if you deign to eat tonight!"

His voice reverberated through the cemetery and the children scrambled to obey his directive. Jessica had barely taken a step to the left, eyes desperately seeking any token that would not need to be dug from a rotting body.

"Oh!" Erin gasped. The younger girl reeled around, heart in her throat once more.

"What are you squawking about, girl?" Gareth rasped, another trembling cough erupting from his mouth. Erin rose an arm and pointed toward the church. They turned to follow her gaze.

In the time they had spent by the open grave, a lamp had been lit inside the previously somber church, the flicker of light radiating by the window.

"Someone's been there all along!" Erin breathed, her eyes wide. "They're watching us right now!"

"Stop gawking, fools! Run before you're caught!" Gareth snarled, rushing off with his cane in hand. He was a shockingly nimble man for one so large, long legs carrying him effortlessly across the damp grasses.

Jessica remained frozen in place, her body refusing to cooperate with her racing mind.

"Come along, Jessie."

Jake slipped a big hand into hers, yanking her toward the exit and onto the streets beyond. Jessica peered back over her shoulder toward Gareth who had fled in the opposite direction. Their guardian did not pause to ensure they had followed but Erin, who sat close on Gareth's heels, stopped to look for her street siblings.

"Don't fret about them now," Jake growled, pulling Jessica away. "The priest isn't apt to chase us all. We'll be long parted before anyone sees us."

had been a deep red with curls as springy as the stone angel's. It had been a long while since a bath had washed away the caked dirt that clung to her strands, permanently staining them brown, hiding the lice that roamed freely about her scalp.

Stars blinked mockingly as she fumbled for her bearings. Thin lips parted to call out but immediately, she clamped them closed. She could not risk her companions being found, trampling about the graveyard in search of a scrap or coin to trade or sell for a spot of bread.

I'll make do, she told herself bravely. *I just need to keep my wits. What would Gareth do if 'e were me?*

She did not remind herself that Gareth would never find himself in such a precarious situation. He was far too clever for such nonsense.

Vivid blue eyes searched the muddy prison for means of escape. Thankfully, the freshly dug grave was unoccupied, a small blessing that. For all the corpses she had seen in her young life, the sight and smell never quite became commonplace to Jessica's senses.

Small roots protruded through the dirt to offer a solution to her problem.

Scrambling to her feet, Jessica hooked a small hand against one of the twines, straining her aching legs toward freedom. She had not eaten since the previous night, as was the norm. Gareth saved their meals for work well done but the lack of nourishment made Jessica's arms shaky.

I will do this! she thought with intense determination, but God had other plans for her.

The ground was far too slippery to abide her movements and before she had climbed halfway, her fingers weakened against the slick earth, sliding the girl back where she had begun.

A small whimper threatened to escape her mouth but Jessica managed to smother it as she tried again to elevate herself from the open grave. Once more, her efforts were thwarted, her frail limbs no match against nature's defences.

After the third attempt, she did not rise from where she had landed, crumbled in the corner. She willed herself to be calm, to ignore the hysteria creeping up inside her.

This is 'ow I meet God? In the throes of a crime?

Perhaps she would not meet God at all, she reasoned. There were far too many penances for her to pay and she was already halfway to Hell where she was in that moment.

Squeezing her eyes shut, she folded her hands tightly and prayed.

"Dear Lord, 'ave someone find me a'fore I drop dead in the grave meant for another. I beg yer forgiveness for all I've stolen and if Ye should take me tonight, let Erin find the bread I've 'idden so that she and Jake don't go 'ungry. Amen."

Peeking through one eye, she saw no one overhead and again tightened her eyelids, pulling a protective shroud around her.

They won't leave me. Gareth will see I'm not with the others.

Again, it was small consolation to the panicking child who could hear little from her dirt jail. For all she could glean, they had already taken what they could find and were making their way to the roofless house on Elm Street without her.

Minutes evaporated, Jessica's breaths escaping in short, uneven rasps. Time lost sense as the moon lowered in the sky. Tears burned behind her eyelids and she sniffled. Perhaps she would not die but be found by a groundskeeper in the morning where she would be shipped off to an orphanage, never to see her makeshift family again. To young Jessica, it was a fate worse than death.

For a fleeting second, the smell of lavender and rosewater touched her nostrils, a woman's voice singing wordlessly in her ears. Peace stole into her soul as the familiar dream encompassed her. She permitted herself a moment of fantasy, knowing that was precisely what it was, her imagination at work. It was the only means of comfort she could grasp in such a helpless situation.

"Stop your bloody snivelling!" The poke of the walking stick against her shoulder forced Jessica's eyes open, head dropping back to meet Gareth's irked expression. "You'll rouse attention with your mewling, you fool!"

A fusion of relief and concern gnarled inside her uneasy stomach. Gareth's low hiss was a hair of comfort but there would undoubtedly be reprimand later. Erin and Jake appeared at his side, their faces horrified to see the girl in the hole. Erin's sooty eyes widened, tousled black hair falling over her heart-shaped forehead as she strained to reach for Jessica with her bare hands.

"Are you hurt?" Erin cried, ignoring Gareth's deepening scowl.

"Hush your mouth, girl!" Gareth growled, tapping at Erin to sit back against the lip of the grave. He readjusted the stick in his hands, extending his arm for Jessica to reach the end. Grateful for the rescue, Jessica curled her fingers over the smooth wood and allowed Gareth to lift her out. He all but tossed her aside, untangling his beloved walking stick from her grasp. At once, Jake and Erin flanked the child, studying her mud-streaked face for evidence of injury.

Jessica eyed her guardian warily, flinching as he dug his stick back into the dirt to glower at her. Leaning forward on the knob, his hands piled upon each other, he spat to the side before running his tongue over crooked, yellowing teeth.

"Have you lost your senses, running headlong into a grave?" Gareth growled. "Is this your way of seeking attention?"

Jessica shook her head vehemently.

"I couldn't see!" Jessica protested. "I 'aven't been 'ere a'fore to know where I was stepping!"

"That's no excuse!"

"Ye cannot fault 'er for a misstep," Jake said jumping to Jessica's defence. "None of us know this cemetery. It could have 'appened to any of us, Pa."

Gareth's eyes became slits of anger, his brows creating a vee shape.

"You've eyes, haven't you?" Gareth was unmoved by Jake's lamentation, his massive form looming over the trio. In contrast to the moonlight, his russet brown hair appeared black, hints of white strands illuminated against the beams. He opened his mouth to speak again but an untimely cough sprayed from his lips before he could muster another word. The rattling fit passed in seconds as the children waited with bated breath. When he had recomposed himself, Gareth leaned in closer to glare at Jessica with chilled blue eyes. "You're bloody lucky no one but me heard your weeping."

He roused a valid point, but Jessica realised she was not concerned about being caught. Her thoughts were already on Elm Street and Gareth's temperament when they arrived.

Jake shared the same dark thoughts.

"I'm sure 'e won't let us eat tonight," Jake muttered, hurrying along with Jessica firmly in his grasp. She panted and ran, her holed shoes slowing her down against the sodden ground but Jake permitted no languidness.

"Come on, 'urry up, Jessie!" he snapped with Gareth's impatience. Yet he did not release her, his grip tightening as if he worried she might slip away through is fingers. Gareth had never held onto her like that.

"What do ye mean he won't feed us? It isn't our fault there was someone in the rectory," she huffed. Jake snorted, running his other hand through a tuft of grimy hair. Jessica imagined that his hair, like hers, had once been much lighter in colour.

"You've lived among us too long to be such a babe in the woods, Jessie," he grumbled. "Pa looks for any excuse not to share his food. Haven't ye figured that out by now?"

Jessica was aghast, a stab of disloyalty piercing her chest at Jake's unkind words. Gareth had saved them, protected them, kept them safe when no one else in the world had wanted them.

"Yes 'e will," she squeaked, her little breath rough as she struggled to oblige his long strides. "I know 'e'll feed us!"

Abruptly, Jake stopped, his dark eyes storming over. Gasping for breath, Jessica also stopped, thankful for the moment to rest. The church was still in view but the light was no longer visible from where they stood. No one ran after them, their fist waving, demanding they stay put. They were out of harm's way—for the moment.

Jessica's frame still trembled from the tumble she had taken, her belly tight with hunger. She silently prayed that Jake's prophecy was wrong. She could not go another day without food.

"Did you take anything from the graveyard?" he demanded.

"I fell!" Jessica complained, her cheeks tinging crimson.

"Before you fell?" he growled. There was a modicum of hope in his dark eyes, and she loathed to diminish it. Jessica swallowed and stared up solemnly, shaking her head.

"No…"

Jake grimaced.

"Nor did we," Jake spat, again snatching her back toward the wrought-iron fence, any semblance of faith evaporating from his face. "I'm telling you, 'e won't feed us."

Jessica fell silent, her little feet rushing to keep pace with Jake. A rumble of thunder in the distance spoke of impending rain. She wondered if she should tell Jake of her secret end of bread, hidden amongst the tattered blanket she used to sleep. Jessica had found it in a rubbish pile, half green with decay on the very same night that Erin had lost her boot.

"We won't starve," Jessica piped up, hoping to alleviate his sour expression. "I've some bread if Pa doesn't give us supper tonight."

Jake scoffed but cast her a sidelong look of affection.

"I do!" Jessica promised. "It's 'idden in me spot!"

"Then it won't be there anymore." Jake sighed, squeezing her fingers gently. "The rats 'ave surely 'ad it, stupid."

Disappointment clutched Jessica's heart as she recognised the truth to Jake's words.

I know 'e'll feed us, she insisted optimistically but as fat droplets of rain began to pelt from the sky, Jessica could not shake the sense that God was telling her otherwise. It was bound to be a long and terrible night.

CHAPTER 2

*H*enry's head jerked upward with a start, verdant eyes blinking as he took note of his surroundings. The candle which he had been reading by, long since extinguished, the plumes of smoke vanished like his attention at the books before him.

I must have nodded off, he thought with some embarrassment, but it did not linger as he realised something had woken him and there was no one in the room.

A chill enshrouded the rectory, his simple black shirt and slacks doing little to block the draft that crept through the stone walls of the church. There was no clock to determine how long he had been asleep at his posting but Henry reasoned it was best he did not know. He determined it was late, the high moon beams dictating that he had missed his evening meal long ago. He reached for the blanket draped along the back of the chair and shook his head as if to clear the cobwebs of his mind.

The examinations were upon him, forcing Henry to burn his own candle at both ends as he strove to achieve his priesthood. A young man of sixteen, Henry hailed from a gentry family, his strong features and noble bearing evidence of a good upbringing. He was the first of his kin to seek a career within the church but he was certain it was his calling. Even now, he thought of the remarkable act of kindness he had seen that had inspired his studies, the image forever etched in the back of his mind.

A distinct voice caught his attention and the remnants of sleep evaporated as Henry tensed, reaching for a nearby lamp to light, the blanket falling away from his broad shoulders.

The shuddering glow illuminated the interior of the chapel, causing Henry to strain his neck toward the stained glass beyond. He could see little through the gaily painted panes but his senses alerted him to movement beyond the walls even if he could not fully bear witness to what was happening outside.

He rose, taking the lamp with him to venture from the cool interior, a fission of goosebumps erupting over his skin. At that hour of the night, he did not much care for the notion of traipsing about the graveyard, but he could not very well ignore the noises.

Foolish superstitions, he chided himself, pushing open the heavy, oak door leading outside. *The dead are sleeping. Only the living create sounds.*

For a moment, he paused, inhaling the ozone filling the air. Rain was upon them, hardly uncommon for the area but on this night, it seemed rife with foreboding. Again, he scolded himself for such ridiculous thoughts and plunged onward to investigate.

The moon continued to glow above, clouds hovering near but not on top of the luminous orb. Henry pivoted his head to the right and then left, searching for signs of what had roused him from his ill-timed nap.

The massive stone angel stole his gaze, Henry's eyes resting fully upon the statue with reverential awe. For all the time he had spent in the church, he had never quite overcome the sensation of respectful fear that the statue instilled in him. He could not say for certain what it was about the idol. They were a common sight in most cemeteries, even if this one was much larger than most. Perhaps it was that fact alone which startled Henry every time. St. Michael's was not a prosperous church, yet the angel was quite costly. It marked the grave of one David Hawthorne, cherished husband, doting father—or so the plaque read, coupled with his birth and death dates. Mr Hawthorne had been deceased a mere five years but little else was known about the man—at least not to Henry. He had not thought to ask Father Thompson or anyone else about the oddly placed statue despite the minutes he had spent studying it. Henry had perused the etchings many times over the past months, studying it for clues about who else Mr Hawthorne may have been. To his knowledge, no one had ever come to visit the angel with its extended finger, wings extended gloriously as if to float up to Heaven upon God's word. There were no Hawthorne's that Henry could think of who regularly attended services.

Who were you, Mr Hawthorne? How did you come to be buried here?

It was not the first time the query had entered his mind but tonight, it caused Henry a shiver of dismay followed by a rash of goosebumps over his arms. The young man rubbed his left hand over his arm, stepping forward to further investigate the noises he had heard previously, lamp raised to his forehead. Could they have been from the ghost of Mr Hawthorne?

Enough with that nonsense! You are a man of sixteen, not a boy of six!

A drop of rain splattered on his face, causing Henry to jump. Inhaling, he mocked himself silently, venturing out through the white, picket gate toward the tombstones. Fresh footprints in the mud told him he had only just missed the source of his chagrin but when he turned back toward the church, his heart leapt into his throat. A shadowy figure glided towards him, face hidden beneath a wide brimmed hat. Horrified, Henry raised his lamp, the faint glow illuminating the face of the nearing spirit.

"Father Thompson!" Henry choked, sheepishness overtaking him as he realised it was his mentor who loomed in the darkness.

"Mr Allen," the old priest responded, a note of dryness to his tone. "You look as though you've seen a ghost."

Henry was suddenly grateful for the low light, his blush well hidden from Father Thompson's astute eyes. The boy chuckled nervously.

"Where is your lamp?" Henry asked worriedly. "It's dark and you'll surely stumble among the graves."

Father Thompson scoffed, tipping his head back to stare at Henry reprovingly. His wide-brimmed hat fell to slightly obscure his face once more.

"I've wandered these grounds longer than most of the spirits, Mr Allen. After forty years at this church, I have no need to waste precious whale oil on trivial matters."

Henry parted his lips to ask why the old man had found himself out at that hour when the priest explained himself.

"I searched your dormitory when you did not appear for the evening meal. I thought perhaps you had taken a constitution but when you did not return, I found myself concerned."

"I was studying in the church," Henry explained, nodding toward the building at their back. "I must have lost all sense of time."

He did not volunteer that he had inadvertently fallen asleep. Father Thompson nodded approvingly.

"It does make for a better connection to God Almighty in His house. However, it does not explain why you are trampling about a wet graveyard at this hour of the night."

"I heard sounds," Henry said quickly, his eyes traveling back over the landscape. Whomever had been there was long gone by now, their footprints washing away as the rain fell harder over the pair. A dampness formed at the base of Henry's neck, sending another shudder down his spine. Father Thompson noticed at once.

"Come along now, before you catch your death," the priest intoned, gesturing for Henry to follow him back toward the church.

"But what of the noises?" Henry protested. Father Thompson paused and shook his head.

"Whoever it was has surely gone by now," he reassured Henry. "There's no need to chase through the rain unnecessarily. You will only serve to make yourself ill."

Father Thompson turned back toward the church and with a final glance about, Henry hurried to keep stride with the older man. Inside the rectory, Henry shook the rain drops from his body and addressed Father Thompson.

"Who could it have been?" Henry asked worriedly. "It's hardly a time to be visiting loved ones."

"Eh?" Father Thompson sat heavily at the desk Henry had previously occupied. He eyed the boy's books through his peripheral vision.

"In the cemetery. Who could have been out there?"

The old man shifted his eyes back toward Henry, a pitying look in his eyes.

"Have you learned nothing these past months?" he asked, leaning forward to entwine his weathered hands in his lap. "You undoubtedly roused a vagrant, seeking shelter for the night."

A stab of shame pierced Henry's chest but before he could dwell upon his regret, Father Thompson added, "Or a grave robber."

Aghast, Henry gaped.

"A grave robber?" he sputtered. "Truly?"

Father Thompson was unfazed by his shock.

"We've seen but a few thieves," he conceded. "This area is not renowned for its riches. That is not to say that it could not occur. London grows by the day as does the stench of poverty and disquiet."

Immediately, Henry thought of Mr Hawthorne and his costly stone angel.

"How despicable," Henry murmured, appalled at the thought of the dead being desecrated in such hideous fashion.

"Desperate souls do desperate things," Father Hawthorne intoned. "'Tis a problem as old as time itself."

"I cannot fathom the notion," Henry grumbled, his head again craning toward the stained-glass windows. Of course, there was nothing for him to see even if he were able to penetrate the frosted glass with his vivid, green eyes.

"You will come to fathom many notions," Father Thompson replied prophetically. "I have come to understand the deepest crevices of human suffering in my years."

"Theft of the dead is no way to alleviate suffering," Henry huffed. "I won't abide it. On church ground no less!"

Father Thompson did not display the same passion for the subject.

"There is little to be done about such things, Mr Allen. I reckon that you are best off studying, not concerning yourself with criminal matters."

"I will do both," Henry announced, an idea formulating in his head. Father Thompson arched a bushy eyebrow warily.

"How's that now?"

"I spend my nights studying here as it is. I will keep vigilant watch on the graveyard henceforth. No one will touch the graves of the rested."

For the first time, Father Thompson appeared bewildered. His bird-like jaw twitched nervously as he shook his snow-white head of hair, strands catching at his collar, contrasting with the charcoal of his frock.

"There's no need for such measures, Mr Allen. Whomever they are were likely frightened off by your lamp and won't see fit to return anytime soon."

"More the reason that they may return," Henry insisted. "If I frightened them away before they had finished their thieving. They will be—"

"The notion is foolhardy," Father Thompson interjected. Henry blinked, mildly stung by the older man's tone. The priest caught sight of Henry's expression and quickly softened his words. "I fear that these robbers are oftentimes armed and irrational. It serves no good to confront men like that."

Henry balked but his resolve was steadfast. He thought of Mr Hawthorne, his final resting place disrupted by ruffians while he sought eternal sleep.

All while I sit fifty paces away? I won't have it.

"I'll proceed with caution," Henry reassured his mentor. Father Thompson sighed heavily and rose from the rickety chair, ambling toward the cupboards set above the consecration wine.

Henry arched an eyebrow. He had never known Father Thompson to sneak a nip but he was aware that other priests did not mind sharing in the communion wine during non-service hours. His suspicions were quickly suppressed when the man opened a cupboard, reaching deep inside. A small frown formed on his face as he twisted his fingers about, clearly in search of something. Henry found himself fearing for the man's fingertips, lest a mouse mistake his wrinkled digits for bits of food.

"May I ask what you're doing, Father?" Henry asked tentatively. Father Thompson's face lit up as he yanked something from the depth of the shelves. Henry gasped aloud as the priest whirled about, his ivory mane flying to display a pistol in his hand. The boy reeled back in shock, hands up in mercy as the priest began to chuckle.

"Good heavens, son," the old man snorted. "Did you truly believe I'd fire upon you? Get a hold of your wits, boy."

Relief fused with wariness in Henry's gut and he cast his mentor a look of confusion.

Why is there a gun in a house of God?

Father Thompson was quick to explain.

"I merely wanted you to know that this pistol is nearby, should you ever find yourself facing trouble."

Henry's eyes widened to the same shape as the base of the brass candleholder on the desk.

"Oh…I don't…" he mumbled, awe and fear encompassing him. It was akin to the feeling he had experienced in the cemetery, a healthy reverence touching him. As a boy, before Henry had pledged his life to God, his father had allowed the child to join in on his hunting excursions with the men. But to fire upon a living, human soul for no other purpose than protection of property? It seemed overzealous.

"You needn't appear so concerned, Henry," Father Thompson chuckled again, losing all formality now that they shared in a secret.

"I-I simply cannot understand why such an object would exist inside the walls of God's house," Henry blurted forth before he was able to stop himself. The priest laughed, the displaced sound echoing through the airy walls of the rectory.

"To scare off the foxes, of course," he chortled when he had managed to catch his breath. "What other reason is there?"

THE LITTLE STONE ANGEL 21

"Foxes?" Henry echoed, a twinge of relief touching him. "Do we have many?"

"About as many as grave robbers," Father Thompson quipped. "They are sometimes apt to dig at the shallower graves, in search for food."

That is nearly as shameful as robbing the graves! Henry thought indignantly. Father Thompson returned the gun to where he had found it, shutting the closet behind him.

"Such is nature, Henry. Foxes, mice, humans—we are all merely animals abiding by our most basic instincts —survival."

"As humans, we have a better capacity to control our sinful urges," Henry mumbled, daunted by the talk of marred corpses.

"One would hope," Father Thompson chirped. Henry managed a small smile but his heart pounded inside his chest. "I maintain that it is a fool's errand to lie in wait for these men."

The man wiggled a bushy, white eyebrow. "Do reconsider. I rather enjoy having you here. I'd not like to visit you in the cemetery."

For a moment, Henry vied to recant his offer, the firearm giving him pause.

There's no need to announce my cowardice aloud. Father Thompson is undoubtedly correct. The robbers won't return and I'll have no occasion to fret.

"I should be on my way. The hour is late and my weary bones curse me," the priest remarked, moving toward the wooden doors of entry. "I fear that sleep is a luxury I cannot ignore at my age."

Henry hurried to see him out, offering a lantern to guide his way back toward the dormitories. Father Thompson waved his hand impatiently, scooping his stovepipe hat from one of the pews where he had left it upon entry.

"No need, Mr Allen," he averred. "I will find my way."

He replaced his brimmed hat on his head and marched into the rain with far more agility than a man of his age should boast. Henry watched him disappear into the darkness before ducking back inside the church, securing the doors with the beam and bars. It was the first time Henry had ever thought to lock the door of the church. Yet as the chill clung to his tired bones, the young man had a perilous feeling that it would not be his last.

CHAPTER 3

*A*s Jake had predicted, the rats had fully eaten the end of Jessica's secret stash of bread. She stared helplessly at the crumbs, tangled through her blanket, with mounting frustration. All the way back to the half-formed shopfront, her tongue jutted out to lick her lips, tasting at the freshly driving rain to wet her dry mouth. The small bit of fresh water against a parched mouth was no great relief but it was enough to sustain the girl, the thought of her hidden morsel keeping her from collapsing on the streets.

Now, her hopes were fully dashed.

"What is keeping him?" Erin muttered as she hunkered in her own small corner. Bare feet peeked through the rips of her blanket, toes wriggling to keep heat with the movement. Sighing, Jessica wrapped herself in the frayed quilt and strained to hear voices beyond the stone that separated the girls from the males. The top part of the wall was as exposed as the sky above them, the small portion of roof holding enough to block the children from soaking in the rain without avoiding its dampness. The blanket Jessica clung to was sodden already. It would be better to sleep without it, rather than permit the dampness to absorb into her bones.

"Do you hear what they're saying?" Erin pressed, leaning forward, her grey eyes wide. Jessica shook her head.

"No…" she paused, sensing it was not the best time to ask but her rumbling belly spoke for her. "Do ye think Pa'll let us eat tonight?"

Erin balked at the question, her sallow expression waxing more.

"Jake says 'e won't because we didn't find any trinkets t' sell."

Erin's eyes hardened and she turned away, her mouth becoming a fine line.

"We'll make do, just as always," she muttered. The answer was not what Jessica had hoped to hear but she knew better than to pepper the girl with questions. Although Erin was more patient than Jake and Gareth, her nerves were often fraught.

A low grunt caught the younger's girl's ears and her head whipped around to peer over the low, broken wall. She was far too slight to properly see but it had sounded like Jake.

"Get down from there this instant!" Erin hissed, yanking Jessica back to the floor. Jessica cowered and Erin's eyes fixed solemnly on her face, her own expression softening—only slightly. "Unless you want Pa to give you a walloping too."

Jessica had often marvelled at Erin's well-spoken ways. The girl pondered who Erin may have once been, before Gareth found her. Jessica could not recall a time when the slender, sloe-eyed girl had not been there but that meant little. She had no more recollection of her own life than Erin did of hers.

When she was smaller, more naïve, Jessica liked to pretend that she was a noble-born girl who had been mistakenly lost. In her mind's eye, she envisioned herself a lady, sought by her parents the Duke and Duchess of the whole of London.

Gareth disarmed her of that notion the moment he caught wind of her fantasy.

"You were left in the gutter, like rubbish," he snorted when Jessica offered her explanation of how she had come to be in his care. "Half-naked without so much as a scrap of food to see you through. I assure you, a princess you are not. You should consider yourself blessed that I came across you or else you'd surely have perished. Perhaps I should've left you behind, ungrateful brat you've become."

Jessica realised that the scenario she imagined seemed unlikely as she grew older, but Erin could easily have been such a girl with her smooth, pale skin and proper manners. It was a small wonder that Gareth preferred her to the uncouth ways of Jessica and Jake.

"Is that what you want? A walloping?" Erin pressed, bringing the younger girl back to the inhospitable stone walls of her reality. Jessica shook her head vehemently but before she could utter a word, footfalls met her ears. The girls tensed in unison, eyes trailing toward the sound. Jake appeared at the doorway, his face bruised against the light of his candle. Jessica swallowed her upset, the streaks of blood around his eyes twisting her stomach. No matter how many times she saw her siblings in this state, she could not quite grow accustomed to it.

"Let me have look." Erin sighed, rising from her place to tend to Jake. He waved her off but before a word was exchanged, Gareth appeared behind them. He chewed the last of whatever had been in his mouth, eyes narrowing.

"Why are you still awake?" he demanded, glowering at Jessica. "I won't hear your complaints on the morrow about your tiredness if ye won't sleep."

"I'm 'ungry," Jessica replied promptly. "Won't we 'ave supper?"

Erin inhaled sharply and cast Jessica a warning look.

"Supper?" Gareth echoed mockingly. "Have you taken leave of your senses?"

Disappointment but not surprise surfaced inside Jessica. It was the response she had expected but it burned to hear it all the same. She willed her stomach to stop flipping.

"What did you contribute to our family today?" Gareth went on, ambling closer toward the girl. "What did ye do to earn any supper?"

Jessica hung her head, darting her eyes away.

"Eh?" Gareth demanded. "Why should ye eat when you haven't paid your way?"

"I shouldn't," Jessica whispered, unable to meet his furious glare.

"You'll do well to remember this for tomorrow when we return to St. Michael's," Gareth growled. "This time without rousing the attention of the priests."

All three children gaped at him in dismay.

"You'd have us return to the same graveyard so soon after we were almost caught?" Erin croaked. "Is that wise?"

Gareth's frown deepened in the shadowy darkness. To Jessica, he seemed more creature than man against the dim light and rain. Jake's candle extinguished, the flame caught by the downpour before he could shelter it.

Now they all sat in the darkness, not even the moon providing illumination but it did not hide the anger in Gareth's face.

"Wise?" he repeated, spittle flying from his mouth. Jessica saw bits of food twined with his saliva, causing her stomach to flip once more. She found herself focussed more on his spittle than his rantings, one more commonplace than the other. "Wise would have been you fools returning with something to sell! Wise would not have been you falling into that hole and seeing us caught! Wise is not to question the only man who has seen you safe and fed!"

His voice carried over the rain and Jessica cowered. His eyes seemed empty cavities and she had no illusions of what might come if she continued to question him. Hastily, she looked to her hands.

"Get to bed, the lot of you," Gareth snarled, answering Jessica's question without directly responding. There would be no supper that night.

Gareth whirled and stomped away toward his section of the run-down building. Once, it had been a small shopfront, a seamstress or tailor of sorts. The remnants of cloth and sewing thread had proven useful to patch some of the holes in the children's clothing but little else about the spot was useful. Poor construction and weather-wear had demolished the shop to a mere pile of stones and mortar. For now, it was home but like all the other abandoned locations the family had found in the past, it would be temporary. They would scour the area for whatever goods to be found and move along, as always.

Gareth's room was the only one with a full roof, protecting him from the elements. As usual, he had found the most comfortable area for himself as the children made do with whatever else they could find. He often invited Erin to join him, but she refused, citing Jessica as her reason, and igniting Gareth's irritation. The younger girl wished she had been offered such luxuries and she often urged Erin to join Gareth's more comfortable quarters.

"Ye should go with 'im! I reckon it's warmer and there may even be cake!"

"You should shut your stupid mouth," Erin fired back. "And not trouble yourself with matters of which you know nothing."

Tonight, Gareth made no such offer to Erin.

"I'm 'ungry," Jessica moaned. "And the rats ate me bread."

"Stop yer snivelling," Jake growled, flopping down in the space between the two girls. He reached for the satchel strewn across his sinewy frame. Jessica strained forward, eyes widening as her companion pulled something from the depth of his bag. From his place across the shop, Gareth began to cough, the spastic rumblings echoing through the space.

The children tensed, waiting for the sound to finish before Jake turned his attention back to Jessica.

"Eat this and shut yer mouth," he snapped, throwing something she could not see toward her. Eagerly, Jessica snatched it up, realising it was a piece of half-dried pork belly.

"Where did ye find this?" Jessica asked, her eyes growing in awe.

"Does it matter?" Jake barked. Jessica admitted it did not. She put it to her mouth but hesitated, looking toward her siblings.

"Ye've got nothing te eat," she murmured, extending her hands back toward the teenagers for them to partake also. Erin pressed her lips as Jake snorted. They shook their heads in unison.

"Go on," Jake insisted, averting his stare. "Weren't ye just whinging about being 'ungry? It's getting wet in the rain, right?"

Jessica bit on her lower lip, eyes darting between her urchin siblings. She did not feel right about eating when they had nothing, but arguing with the pair together was more futile than fighting with Gareth.

"Bring yourself here," Erin muttered, gesturing for Jake to draw closer. The boy started to shake his head but Erin did not permit his refusal. Scrambling up from her place, she grabbed his hand and pulled him toward the cold ground. Reluctantly, he allowed himself to be yanked downward and Erin peered intently at his fresh cuts as Jessica took her first bite of the chalky pork.

Strings of meat clung to her teeth, and she chewed relentlessly, noting the slight tang to the otherwise tasteless piece. The effort caused soft enamel to crunch in her mouth, forcing her to slow her munching.

"What did you say that made him so angry?" Erin muttered under her breath but Jessica's astute ears picked up the whisper. For all her frailness, the girl had ears and eyes of otherworldly proportions.

"Nothing!" Jake snapped, folding his arms defiantly over his chest. "I don't need to say a word te make 'im furious."

"You would be wise to keep that sharp tongue of yours in place," Erin retorted, using the end of her quilt to wipe away at Jake's injuries.

"Me tongue isn't sharp," he insisted. "Pa's just looking for a reason te behave like a monster."

"Then don't give him one!"

Jessica tried to speak but the bite she had taken refused to be broken down in her small mouth. She continued to chew, ignoring the foulness of the rising taste. It would not be the first time she had eaten spoiled meat. She only wished she had a cup of water with which to wash it down.

Her eyes darted around the space hopefully for a collection of rainwater but there was nothing nearby and ultimately, Jessica was forced to choke down the hardened chunk without properly breaking it down. She gagged and choked, causing Erin to pound on her back.

"What did you do?" the older girl demanded, as Jessica gasped and coughed.

"Shh!" Jake hissed. "Ye want te wake Pa?"

Jessica clamped a hand over her own mouth, still sputtering as Erin retreated to her sleeping spot, confident that the younger girl was not in the throes of death.

"Sorry," Jessica squeaked, eying the remaining piece of meat in her hands. After the lengths she had gone to consume the first bite, she was wary of taking another. Her gut lurched, reminding her that it might be the last morsel she ate for another day or two. She took another chomp, this bit much smaller.

"We shouldn't go back te that graveyard," Jake mumbled. "Not yet."

"Is that what earned you a thrashing?" Erin growled, understanding Jake's injuries. "You should know better than to question his plans."

"It's stupid, right?" Jake insisted. "Only a dimwit would return te a spot where we narrowly missed being caught."

"Only a dimwit would argue with Pa," Erin countered. "We know the spot now. We'll be in and gone before anyone will be the wiser."

"Tell that te this one." He threw a thumb over his shoulder toward Jessica who flushed in humiliation. "She ran headlong into a hole."

Jessica's mouth was too full to protest her innocence.

"Leave her be," Erin grouched, cleaning away the last of Jake's blood with her blanket. "Off you go and rest up. It'll be dawn soon."

Jake frowned but he appeared much calmer after Erin's reprimand.

"Yes," he conceded, slipping away from Erin's pallet to curl up on the floor near the doorway. There was no longer a door in the frame but Jake slept across the threshold like a dog on guard. He had no blanket and cupped his calloused hands under his temple before closing his eyes.

Jessica continued to gnaw on the shoe leather in her mouth, contemplating Jake's concerns. She, too, believed that it was unwise to return to the church and cemetery.

The second bite finally crept down Jessica's throat and she tentatively parted her lips.

"Erin?"

"What is it, Jessie?"

"What'll happen if we're caught?"

"What?"

"What if we return on the morrow and the priest finds us," Jessica explained. "What'll become of us?"

There was a long silence.

"Will we get locked up in jail?" Jessica pressed. "Will we go te an orphanage?"

All of the terrible thoughts she had at the graveyard resurfaced in a flurry of queries. She knew what Gareth had warned of cruel nuns in draughty orphanages, fear of coppers, and a life worse than what they had now. Gareth had a plan for them all, "A beautiful life," waiting for them when they were old enough to work and tend a farm which Gareth would provide for them all.

"Erin?" Jessica squeaked when she did not respond. "What'll—"

"Go to sleep, Jessie!" Her voice was taut and left no room for protest. It was clear that Erin did not want to consider Jessica's concerns.

"Oh all right."

She silently admitted it was for the best. A queasiness had followed her peppering of questions. Bile rose into her throat but Jessica swallowed quickly, forcing down the acrid liquid lest she spray it all over. It was sure to annoy her companions, even if it had happened before to all of them.

Closing her eyes, she willed away the ill-feeling in her stomach, waiting for the staple of meat to settle. She was sure that once the foreign sensation of nourishment eased, she would not feel the urge to vomit. Instead, she focussed on their daunting task for the following day.

Everything will go well. Pa knows best. I know 'e wouldn't lead us astray.

CHAPTER 4

"Up and at the day, lazy bones!"

A worn boot poked at Jessica's form and she raised her head sluggishly. The rain had stopped, and sunshine filled the holed cracks of the shopfront, but the sight of the rays blinded Jessica, filling her head with a terrible throbbing. Cotton filled her throat but when she attempted a cough, her stomach flipped violently. She moaned softly, squeezing her eyes closed.

"Not yet," she mewled.

"Come along, Jessie," Erin insisted. "Pa was expecting us on the ports this morning. A shipment's arrived from Spain, or the like, I've heard."

Jessica's limbs refused to cooperate, her bones heavy and exhausted.

"I'm too weary te pick pockets this morn," Jessica mumbled. "Let me sleep."

"Nonsense," Erin insisted. "And it isn't morning anymore. Jake and Pa went to market. They're expecting us at the docks, now. Move your rump, Jessica."

Jessica tried to shake her head but Erin had already pulled away her damp blanket.

"I won't tell you again," Erin snapped. "I won't go alone amongst all those men and Pa is still sore about what transpired last night."

She eyed the piece of meat that Jessica had not consumed, tucked near her ear. Jessica was too weak to hide it, meeting Erin's reproving look.

"You didn't finish," she chided. "That was all for you."

"I couldn't swallow it," Jessica wheezed.

"I'll find you a spot of bread," Erin promised, cajolingly. "But you must get up now, Jessie."

The mere notion of food rushed more bile into Jessica's mouth but she had no choice but to oblige Erin's orders. The older girl was not apt to leave her in peace until she complied. She slowly sat up, a wave of dizziness consuming her.

It was hardly an uncommon feeling. Tiredness and general malaise were standard to little Jessica, the life on the street preparing her for any amount of possible ailments but she could not help but feel she was worse off than usual. Sleeping so late was not typical behaviour but she couldn't will herself to move much faster. Her body half-slumped, determined to lay back down, but Erin's annoyed tone stopped her.

"Jessie!"

"I'm coming," Jessica mumbled, reaching for her tattered shoes. "Give me a moment."

Erin cast her a final, warning look before gliding out of the broken quarters, her long, black mane streaming behind her. Jessica waited for her to exit before slipping her hand into the one good toe of her shoe, withdrawing the small, folded page inside.

On this day, it was a small consolation to realise she had not lost the paper which Jessica had kept in her shoe for longer than she could remember. It was not as though Jessica could read any of the uneven markings she had copied painstakingly but the page represented something to the girl that even she did not understand. Most mornings, it was a relief to see the piece, the one constant in her life when all else was so uncertain. Yet today, nothing could overcome the heavy fog blocking her thoughts.

Sliding the paper back into her footwear, Jessica's feet followed and she rose to use a nearby pot to relieve herself. The rank smell did not usually faze the girl, the fusion of urine, decaying rats, and faeces commonplace to her nostrils. The rush of vomit to her throat stunned her as she stumbled toward the doorway, pulling down on her weather-beaten skirts.

"Will you cease with your dallying?" Erin grabbed her arm and pulled the girl out of the room. "What has gotten into you today? First Jake with his insolence and now you?"

Erin did not want to hear Jessica's complaints, nor did the younger girl have strength to voice them. She fumbled along the cobblestone streets of East London, following her counterpart toward the Greenland Docks.

"We're already tardy, Jessie," Erin growled as they neared, nodding toward a slew of other urchins who had invaded the territory. "There'll be nothing left for the taking if you linger much longer."

Erin's concerns were only half-valid. The ports were ever-filled with sailors and merchants, coming and going from various parts of the world. In another time or place, Jessica may have found the seaways enchanting, the ships loaded with untold fortunes, the crews rife with tales of nautical monsters and faraway lands. Yet today, the stench of dead fish and saltwater merely fuelled Jessica's unrest.

"Hurry up, Jessie!" Abruptly, Erin stopped her rushing to look at the smaller girl. "Are you unwell?"

Instinctively, Jessica shook her matted hair, the movement adding to her distress. Gareth had no use for children who did not earn their keep and she would not disappoint him, particularly not after the previous night's episode. She could not bear the brunt of his wrath when she was already feeling so poorly.

"Don't fib, Jessie. You're whiter than a ghost. Come and let me feel your forehead."

Jessica swallowed the excess water in her mouth and shook her head again.

"No, I'm not," she protested. Her sister did not accept her protests. "I-I think that meat was rotten."

Erin grimaced.

"Is that all? Throw it up and be done with it then," she said and sighed, rolling her eyes with annoyance. "Come along."

She pulled Jessica off to the side, ducking them into a laneway between a fish market and carriage shop. The scent of dead marine life only enhanced Jessica's nausea which she suspected was precisely Erin's plan.

"Off you go," Erin pressed, nodding toward the stone of the building. "You know what to do. Finger down your throat and be out with it."

Jessica hesitated but Erin reminded her again of the hour.

"I would prefer not to incense Pa more than he already is. This is no time for modesty, Jessie. You'll feel much better after you've vomited? Get on with it now."

Jessica turned her head and retched, allowing the spoiled contents of her gut to splay over the road and walls.

"Oy! Ye brats!" someone yelled from the street. "Ye'll 'ave to clean that up!"

Tittering, Erin grabbed Jessica's hand and rushed her out the other end of the alley, pushing her into the crowd before they could be chased. After weaving through a lot of dock vendors, the girls again stared at one another. Jessica panted, spitting out the rest of the saliva in her mouth.

"Are you feeling better then?" Erin demanded. Jessica admitted that she did feel slightly improved but her muscles still constricted and her throat was filled with cotton. The sun against her head did little to alleviate the incessant pounding within.

"Yes," Jessica lied. "Much better. Where are we te meet the others?"

Relieved, Erin led the way toward the River Thames and Jessica struggled to keep herself together. Erin did not need to tend to a sick child anymore than Gareth needed to be down a body for that day.

I merely need te make it another few hours before I'm back in me bed.

She was sure she had been through worse already. She could certainly manage another day.

༶

The mild relief that Jessica had garnered at the docks did not remain for long. By the time Gareth instructed the children back to the shop to prepare for their nightly jaunts, her limbs refused to cooperate again, each arm and leg leaden.

"Jessica, ye need move faster than this!" Jake hissed, pushing her along toward the roadway. "Ye've been sullen and moping all day!"

"Leave her be," Erin chided him. "She's taken ill from the spoiled meat you fed her."

Jake looked abashed by the revelation but Jessica shook her head, aghast that her brother was being reprimanded for his kindness.

"No, I'm not. I'm just tired," she insisted, glancing nervously at Gareth who marched before them, a shovel in his hand. Once more, the moon gleamed brightly overhead but there were few clouds in sight. It promised to be a rainless night for once and Jessica thanked God for small favours.

"Work quickly. Dig and take what you can. I won't stand for distractions again. Am I clear?"

The children had reassured him that they were all in good form, prepared to compensate for their previous mistakes.

Yet every step Jessica took closer to the cemetery, she feared she would fall face-first into the grass.

I mustn't fall. The day is almost done and I'll rest tonight. I'll be better in the morn.

The constant refrain in her head did nothing to better her disposition.

"She's not well enough te work tonight," Jake muttered, eying Jessica through his peripheral vision. "'ow long has she been like this?"

"All day," Erin confessed, also shooting the smaller girl a worried look.

"And ye brought 'er along?" Jake snapped. "What were ye thinking?"

"What will you have me do with her?" Erin hissed back. "Leave her here? If I told Pa, surely he would have made me stay with her. Did you yearn to be alone with him?"

Jessica could think of nothing more she would like than to lay down in the grass, feeling the cool blades against her hot, flushed cheeks. She knew she was running a fever but she dared not tell the others.

Jake balked at the suggestion and pursed his lips, his pace quickening.

"Let's 'urry up and be done with this then."

"Stop yer fussing!" Jessica rasped, a small cough falling from her lips. At the same moment, Gareth abruptly stopped to fall on his walking stick, his own rattling hack overtaking Jessica's. The trio paused, inhaling as they did when he coughed. It was as though they all expected him to drop dead with every grating rack he administered. But as always, the fit passed and Gareth marched onward without so much as a backward glance to ensure his wards followed.

"Ye stop yer sickliness," Jake fired back under his breath in response to Jessica's insistence. She had little response as the church loomed before them, once again halting her in her tracks. She had not realised they had come so far already and the sight of it stole her breath. Nervously, she faltered, Jake and Erin oblivious.

In her mind's eye, Jessica saw the light glowing behind the stained glass of the rectory, a scowling preacher looking to capture them all and damn them to Hell. They had been fortunate the previous night but could they be again?

"Jessie!"

Jake's low hiss forced her forward and she rushed to his side. His shovel was already in the dirt of the first grave he found, much to Gareth's chagrin.

"This one won't have anything worthwhile," he snapped, nodding toward the chipped headstone. "Find a better mark. Fools. Have ye learned nothing in all our years together?"

"There's nothing of value in a place like this." Jake spoke the words under his breath but even in her worsened state, Jessica heard. Her crystalline eyes flipped toward Gareth who had started deeper into the cemetery, searching for an appropriate grave.

Instantly, Jessica's eyes rose toward the stone angel she had seen the night before. For a fleeting second, her sickness was forgotten as she again found herself enthralled by his peaceful face. She never had been granted the opportunity to touch it.

Will I 'ave the chance tonight?

She did not have high hopes for herself.

"This one will do," Gareth announced, his voice barely carrying to where the children stood. Jessica wrenched her eyes away from the statue, relieved that he did not signal for that grave to be unturned.

If we're 'ere long enough, Pa'll eventually turn to that one too, Jessica thought with some regret. But for the time, they fixated on a newer headstone of marble. Jessica was unable to read but she could guess what the words might say.

Elizabeth Winchester, beloved Mother.

Or...

Edgar Lyons, God-fearing husband

Something foolish and trite in comparison to the lives they must have led.

"Don't just stand there, girl. Dig!" Gareth ordered Jessica, again reverting her attention back to the task before them. She dropped to her knees and began to rake at the dirt with her bare hands. Her legs still ached from the fall and climb she had attempted, her eyes glancing toward the now-filled grave in which she had fallen. Surely that would be an easier dig, she reasoned, the soil fresh and the corpse not nearly so decayed.

Jessica gagged, slapping a hand over her mouth.

"Jessie!" Erin sank to her side and reached out to move a strand of hair from her face.

"Get to it!" Gareth thundered, his voice low and menacing. Jessica swallowed quickly and gently pushed Erin away. The shovel met wood and the trio scrambled up to lift the lid of the casket. Again, Jessica retched, the stench of rotting flesh touching her nostrils.

"If you vomit, girl, you'll not hear the end of it," Gareth threatened, eying her with contempt. His threat sobered her some but not enough to ease the nausea inside her.

"Wait up here, Jessie," Erin instructed, pulling her back from the lip of the grave. The children dismantled the body, snatching a wedding ring of gold and similar golden cross before joining Jessica again.

"Lookie!" Gareth whispered gleefully, pointing into the darkness. "Someone's left a body out of its grave!"

All eyes flitted to where Gareth pointed, and Jessica paled even more. In the moonlight, her skin was translucent and she began to tremble from the exertion of digging. Her knees buckled and she held out her hands to steady herself.

A corpse lay, half exposed amongst some low bushes. Jessica was stunned by the grotesque sight.

"What is it doing there?" Erin squeaked, echoing Jessica's silent query.

"I warned you, didn't I?" Gareth retorted. "If we didn't come quickly, others would come first. Now we'll have to take it with us."

It was difficult for Jessica to believe that overnight their stake had been discovered but she was too weak to voice her dubiousness. She had not heard Gareth's suggestion until he ordered Jake forward.

"Quickly now, boy, go get the body."

Stunned, Jake gaped at him.

"Ye mean look it over, don't ye?"

"No, boy. I mean take it. We haven't much time. We'll bring it with us."

Jessica and Erin looked to one another, eyes popping.

"Hurry your bloody hide, boy!" Gareth growled before erupting into an unyielding fit of coughs. Like startled deer, the children looked at one another, unsure of how to proceed.

"Pa!" Jessica cried, forgetting to keep her tone low.

"Hush up, you fool!" Gareth choked between his spasms. Jessica extended a finger to point and Gareth cussed to see the light of a lamp growing closer.

"Get it, boy!" he demanded of Jake, smacking him fully on the back of the head with the full force of his brute strength. "Hurry now!"

"You there!" A man's voice called out, neither booming nor high, but loud and commanding. "Stop what you're doing this instant!"

Jake and Erin rushed toward the fallen body and began to drag it as Gareth ducked into the bushes, guiding them forward.

"Hurry! Hurry! Come along!" Gareth coaxed them.

Fear and sickliness enveloped Jessica, freezing her in her place.

"Come on, Jessie!" Erin hissed. The girl whipped her head around as the figure neared, his lamp flickering wildly as he rushed closer. Gareth had vanished into the shrubbery, Jake and Erin following close behind him. Jessica tried to move

THE LITTLE STONE ANGEL 45

forward but her legs seemed stuck in place. Sweat formed at her brow but she shivered with cold, goosebumps raising on her pale arms.

"Jessie!" Erin cried out again but it was the last Jessica heard of them. Slowly, she turned to confront the irate man who sprinted toward them. Spots of black and white danced in her eyes, freckling the black smock and pants of the young man upon her.

But it was not the clothing worn by the dark-haired man, nor the intense green of his furious eyes that captured Jessica's unwavering attention.

It was the pistol he held, aimed, in his hand.

Dizziness over came her but from somewhere inside, a voice screamed for Jessica to run. She whirled around, one foot moving to dash away. But before she was able to take a single step, another wave of sickness washed through her and this time, she was unable to hold it back. She retched, the terror sweeping through her, knowing that her captor was upon her now.

As she expelled the last of her stomach contents onto a nearby grave, she weakly turned her head, arms raised.

"Don't shoot!" she whispered before falling face-first into the ground as blackness consumed her entirely.

CHAPTER 5

The dream was evasive. There was no scent of lavender or rosewater, no woman's voice humming but Jessica thought it was familiar. She inhaled the sweet smokiness of incense but in her mind's eye, Jessica saw the graveyard, a blackness enshrouding her entirely. She could see little, the moon non-existent here yet she knew her family was present.

Just beyond her reach, across from several open graves stood her family, their backs turned toward her. A scatter of unearthed bodies made a path toward the three as they struggled with another corpse, pulling it toward the bushes.

"Pa!" she cried out. "Jake, Erin, don't leave me!"

The trio turned, their faces an identical mask of ire.

"Who are ye?" Jake demanded, eyes narrowing. "Run along. We 'aven't time to govern a bairn."

"It's me! It's Jessie!" She stepped toward them but they fell back in step, hands up to ward her away. Her foot slipped, lunging her shaking body forward into one of the many open graves that separated her from the others. She tumbled into the pit, crying out as she fell. Dirt piled onto her head, half-burying her where she crouched.

Three faces appeared overhead, peering down at her with pity and annoyance.

"Pa! 'elp me! Throw me yer cane!" she begged.

Gareth grinned ruthlessly, flashing his yellow teeth but he made no move to pull her out this time.

"You didn't earn your keep, Jessie. This is what happens! How many times must I warn ye?"

"Jake!" she sobbed, reaching out for her urchin brother but his face was just as cold as Gareth's, his tangled, filthy hair shaking as he pointed a crooked finger at her.

"Yer too much trouble, Jessie," he intoned flatly. "Ye got us caught."

"Let's go," Erin urged, the first to turn away from the spot. "They'll be upon us and one has a pistol!"

The men backed away, following after her, leaving Jessica to bawl.

"Please!" she howled. "Don't leave me here! Please—"

Her eyes popped open and Jessica jerked upward, her heart racing furiously. Slowly, her surroundings came to light, illuminated by a single flickering candle upon a simple wood nightstand. On the wall directly before her was nothing but a wooden cross and another hung over her head. To her left, moonbeams bounced off the glass of a window but from where Jessica lay, she could not see where the panes overlooked. The scent that had originally touched her nose now overwhelmed her, sinking her tense form back against crisp, clean sheets.

I'm on a bed!

Her eyes widened, her head twisting to look at the spotless planked floor beneath her. Tucked within a simple woollen blanket, she hastily, pushed aside the covering to note with some relief that she still wore her filthy, worn clothing. She had heard tales of children snatched off the streets and sold into lives far worse than she could imagine.

Inherently, she sensed she was inside a church and another wave of panic consumed her. A flood of memories returned to her as she recalled where she had last had her bearings. The sickness she had borne all day lingered but her head was clearer now.

I was caught! The man with the pistol!

Struggling to keep her composure, she strained as the soft wisp of voices met her ears.

"…waking soon," one man said. "I should be at her side lest she grow confused."

"She is quite sickly," another murmured. His voice was gravelly, older than the first but just as gentle. "I will send for Dr Morton when she wakes."

"Perhaps not yet," the first man said quickly. "She will likely be overwhelmed when she awakens. Let us take survey of her first."

Jessica realised they were speaking of her, and she frantically looked about for means of escape.

Pa and Jake and Erin will be worried about me, she thought, blinking rapidly as tears filled her eyes. *Unless they were caught too!*

She dreaded to think of what might happen to the rest of her family.

"Oh! You've woken."

She jerked her head around to take note of the two figures in the open doorway. Instantly, she recognised the younger one as the man with the pistol. Jessica scrambled out of the comfortable, clean bed and pushed herself up against the wall. She looked a creature, the hem of her dress yanked over scabbed, bony knees, arms covering her upper body.

"There, there," the older man cooed, drawing nearer. The bottom of his frock brushed against the floor as he crouched down before her. "There's no need to be alarmed, child. I am Father Thompson. You are safe now."

Jessica turned her head fully away, eying the pair through her peripheral vision. She wanted to ask them about Jake and Erin, to know if her siblings had been found but she dared not speak aloud.

"This is Mr Henry Allen," Father Thompson went on, nodding toward his companion. Jessica's head twisted slowly, taking in the clothing of Mr Allen.

He's not a priest. What's 'e doing 'ere?

"Mr Allen is studying for the priesthood," Father Thompson explained as if reading her innermost thoughts. "Soon, he, too, will be a man of the cloth."

Mr Allen smiled at her and Jessica swallowed her nervousness. She felt like a trapped animal but with fewer defences. Their soft, kind words confused her. They were not the stony-eyed preachers she had envisioned in her mind.

"Why don't you come back to bed, dear girl?" Father Thompson suggested. "You appear to have been ill. How are you faring now?"

He extended a hand toward her, but Jessica did not move, nor did she utter a single word.

"Can you speak?" Mr Allen asked, shuffling forward slowly. "Perhaps she's deaf or mute, Father."

His vivid green eyes were rife with worry but Jessica could not forget the gun he had waved about. She again turned away.

"Come along, child," Father Thompson insisted. "The cold ground will not help your cause. You needn't speak with us if you prefer but we would rather you get well than worse, hm? Why don't you remain silent from the warmth of the bed?"

She glanced at the comfortable mattress, thinking of her cold spot at the shopfront on Elm Street. She would not be here long, she reasoned. Why not make the most of the luxuries she was not apt to see again for a long while?

Reluctantly, Jessica accepted his hand and scurried back into the bed, pulling the covers back over her shivering frame.

"That's better," the old man said, beaming at her. "I daresay your colour is better than when you were found."

Jessica's stomach rumbled loudly, tinging her cheeks pink. Eyes darted from one man to another until Father Thompson spoke again.

"I'll see if I can't find a warm bowl of soup and bread," he suggested, stepping back from the bed. "Perhaps a cup of hot tea too?"

Jessica had never tasted tea before but she did not admit it aloud.

"Mr Allen will watch over you in my absence, won't you, son?"

The younger man nodded, his worry tangible.

"Of course. It would be my pleasure."

Father Thompson saw himself out of the small room, leaving Jessica alone with Mr Allen. He found himself a seat in the single chair, next to the window, leaning forward on his forearms to study her face carefully.

"Can you tell me what you were doing out in the cemetery, all alone?" he asked quietly. "It's no place for a little girl at this hour of night."

A smidgen of relief passed through Jessica as she realised her family had not been apprehended. Her gaze darted away to stare at her dirty hands, still caked with dirt.

"Will you tell me your name?" Mr Allen pressed, albeit gently. Jessica could not help but relax under his stare. There was no sign of anger or aggression, despite the firearm he had carried earlier.

"Where's yer gun?" she rasped. Upon speaking, she noticed how dry her throat was and her question was immediately proceeded with an arid hacking. Mr Allen jumped to his feet, hurrying toward a pitcher of water which sat on a table Jessica had not previously seen. He handed her a cup and Jessica accepted it with trembling hands, sweat forming on her brow. A chill rushed through her body but the water felt cool on her burning insides. Mr Allen reclaimed the cup and placed it on the nightstand.

"Did I frighten you with the pistol?" he asked, genuine regret lacing his words. "That was hardly my intention. I wasn't expecting a child amongst the graves."

Jessica sank back into the pillow, curling her slender frame into the foetal position as she continued to watch Mr Allen with wariness.

"It's safely put away," he went on when she did not respond. "You needn't fret about it."

Jessica swallowed, her head swimming, her eyes growing heavier.

"You're running a fever," Mr Allen told her. "How long have you been ill?"

She shrugged.

"It's nothing," she fibbed bravely. "I've 'ad worse."

Sadness crept over Mr Allen's face.

"Of that I have no doubt," he conceded. "But that doesn't change the fact that you are quite ill now."

"I'll be a'right," she insisted stubbornly. Yet even as she spoke, her stomach flipped and bile rushed to her lips. Hastily, she gulped back the vomit that threatened to spill from her mouth.

"Will you tell me your name? It's only fair as you know mine."

She hesitated.

"I would like to know what to call you," he pushed. "And how to return you to your family."

An image of Gareth's face popped into her mind but her dream resurfaced simultaneously.

Pa will be furious over this.

"Jessica."

"That's a lovely name." He smiled and Jessica's taut shoulders relaxed a little more. "What is your family name, Jessica?"

She shook her head.

"I 'aven't one."

He appeared surprised by her admission.

"Surely you must," he replied. "Everyone has a family name. Perhaps you simply don't recall it."

Jessica shrugged again and darted her eyes away.

"If I 'ave one, I don't know it."

Mr Allen paused pensively, cocking his head to the side. The candlelight gleamed off his dark crown of hair.

"Then may I suggest you give yourself one," he offered. Jessica's jaw dropped and she scoffed at the ridiculous idea.

"I don't think that's 'ow it works," she sniggered. "Ye should know that, being a priest and all."

Mr Allen was not bothered by her jibe.

"Why not? I think in your case, you should choose something that speaks of your desires, your needs. What about something akin to Joy?"

She blinked, mouth still agape.

"Say that again?"

"Jessica Joy. I think that has a truly lyrical sound to it. And it's fitting of you. I see a brightness in your soul."

Jessica scoffed openly but inside, her heart twinged.

Jessica Joy is pleasing. Not fitting in the least but better than no surname at all.

The sound of footfalls turned their heads toward the doorway as Father Thompson returned with a silver tray in his hands. Mr Allen rose to help the older man, standing beside the bed.

"Sit up and eat what you can," he instructed her. "You must keep your strength up if you want to rid yourself of this fever."

Jessica righted herself and allowed the tray to be laid across her lap. The smell of fresh chicken broth made her stomach lurch, the flaky bread end calling to her. Saliva flooded her mouth but this time, it was not laced with sick. She picked up the silver spoon and began to shovel large gulps into her mouth, not minding her manners in the least. Crumbs sprayed across the bed as she gobbled the warm food, ignoring the protests of her uneasy gut.

"Slow down or you'll make yourself sick," Father Thompson warned her. "When did you last eat?"

She thought of the rotten meat that had undoubtedly landed her here but did not respond. The charity in their eyes gnawed at her already. She did not want their pity, starving as she were.

THE LITTLE STONE ANGEL

Jessica paused, gasping for air between bites and Father Thompson reached for the tray which she had entirely demolished.

"That will do for now," he said firmly but kindly. "There is more but you should allow yourself time to digest the food."

Her gut creaked, expanding to make room for the rare meal but she could not eat another bite, much as she yearned to. Mr Allen brushed the mess from the bed and Jessica hung her head sheepishly.

"I soiled yer sheets with me filth," she muttered.

"We can arrange a bath for you," Father Thompson offered. "There are clothing donations at the church. Certainly, I can find something that will fit you—and perhaps a new pair of shoes."

Panicked, Jessica looked toward the ground, searching for her footwear.

Have they found me list? she wondered desperately. *'ave they figured out I'm not merely some wandering orphan?*

She dismissed her concerns, sure that they would not be showing such kindness if they suspected who she truly was, a wicked, evil child who desecrated the dead on a nightly basis. If she were to tell them the truth, they would cast her out without a second's notice, banishing her from God's house—and rightfully so.

Her eyes landed on the shoes, lined side by each but otherwise untouched. They had not found the paper hidden inside.

"No," she mumbled, suddenly insurmountably tired. The heat of the soup had settled into her bones, relaxing her upset stomach and causing a sleepiness she could not avoid. "I-I don't want any of that."

The men exchanged a glance.

"Jessica, we must find your family," Mr Allen told her. "They will be very concerned about you, I'm sure."

She avoided their stares, knowing that she could never allow the priest to meet Gareth and the others. Shame and upset twisted inside her.

"Let us pray," Father Thompson suggested brightly. "God will surely guide us—"

Without warning, Jessica burst into tears. She was mortified at her own reaction, but she could not stop as Mr Allen and Father Thompson gaped at her.

Stupid fools, praying for me wasted soul.

"She is overwhelmed," Mr Allen said quickly, shaking his head as Father Thompson moved to lay his hands on her. "Sleep may be a better remedy than prayer at this moment, Father."

"God is always the remedy," Father Thompson argued but Jessica's sniffling sobs silenced him.

"There, there, Jessica Joy," Mr Allen murmured soothingly. "There's no need to cry. Rest now. We will pray for you ourselves as you sleep."

Jessica wiped her face with her hands and shrunk into the bed, exhaustion taking its toll upon her. Her eyes drooped heavily and she struggled to keep up with their conversation but it was almost impossible as exhaustion overtook her.

"Come, Mr Allen," Father Thompson murmured. "Let's allow the child her rest. We can continue to search for her kin on the morrow."

Gratefully, Jessica snuggled back down against the sheets, allowing her lids to fall and wash away the guilt growing inside her.

"Good night, Jessica Joy," Mr Allen whispered, blowing out the candle but Jessica was already half asleep.

"She cannot be older than nine years of age," Father Thompson muttered from the hall outside the door. "I wish she would permit a bath or clean clothes. She is infested with lice."

"She is clearly afraid and leery of strangers." Mr Allen sighed. "We will try again in the morn but for now, let us pray that she improves."

"Her colour is much better than when she arrived. Perhaps there is hope for her…"

The voices drifted away as did Jessica in the warmth and security of the church.

In the night, hands laid on her forehead and whispers of bible verses touched her ears.

"He called a little child to him and placed the child among them. And he said: 'Truly I tell you, unless you change and become like little children, you will never enter the kingdom of heaven. Therefore, whoever takes the lowly position of this child is the greatest in the kingdom of heaven. And whoever welcomes one such child in my name welcomes me. If anyone causes one of these little ones—those who believe in me—to stumble, it would be better for them to have a large millstone hung around their neck and to be drowned in the depths of the sea.'"

Jessica strained to open her eyes, the now-familiar voice lulling her back into sleep again. Mr Allen remained steadfastly at her side, checking her for signs of improvement until Jessica was again caught up in her favourite dream.

A woman hummed softly, cool dribbles of water raining over the girl's face and body, lavender and rosewater bathing her soul.

"Who are ye?" Jessica asked the faceless woman. She did not reply but with her wordless hymn, trailing long fingers over the softness of her skin.

Another strong hand touched her forehead and this time, Jessica was able to open her eyes, pale dawn sunlight streaming in through the single window.

But she was alone in the room, no sign of anyone to comfort her. It reminded her that she did not belong there, in this consecrated place which she had defiled with her mere presence. She needed to get home to her real family.

CHAPTER 6

Stuffing her feet into the dilapidated shoes, Jessica looked hastily about for signs of Father Thompson or Mr Allen. She winced to see how badly she had stained the clean sheets, the idea of a bath teasing the back of her mind.

Off ye go! she chided herself, knowing she had already taken full advantage of a friendly priest and his pupil. Jessica's shame was palpable as she stole away from the small but cozy room that had housed her better than she had ever known in her young life.

The room had developed a distinctive chill overnight and as she ventured out into the hallway, she realised that she was not in the church but in the dormitories adjacent. Her heart in her throat, she listened for movement but if there were more bodies about, she did not sense them and she seized the opportunity to run before either man could come and check on her. She thought to find a kitchen, perhaps to take a morsel of bread for her travels.

No, 'aven't I stolen enough from this church? she thought, disgusted with herself. *I'm already destined for the pits of 'ell.*

The graveyard looked very different in the daytime, the stone angel not nearly as haunting against a blue backdrop. Temptation drew her toward the statue but she did not dare linger. If the men were to see her, she had no doubt that they would ask her to return and Jessica worried her resolve would not hold when presented with the idea of a hot bath and warm meal again. She could not stay there forever, nor did she want to add to God's wrath for all her countless sins.

Pa will be worried about me, she thought firmly, pushing her frail figure out toward the street. Through her peripheral vision, she half hoped to see Mr Allen come after her, calling her back, but he did not materialise.

Her steps were even, not crippled by stomach cramps or tremors. She could not be sure if her fever had broken but by comparison to the previous night, Jessica felt much stronger. She recalled the dreams, the sound of Mr Allen's voice in her sleep, reading to her.

That was a dream, ye bloody fool. Just like the one with the lavender.

She wove through the East End, ducking through the docks to make her way up toward the shopfront on Elm Street. Dawn continued to creep over the Thames and when Jessica finally found herself amongst her street family, she exhaled a breath she had not realised she had been holding.

Jake lay at the threshold as always, protecting a sleeping Erin within. Jessica moved to climb over him but before she could, a furious voice rang out.

"Where in tarnation have ye been all night?!"

THE LITTLE STONE ANGEL

Jake and Erin sat up in unison as Jessica turned to confront Gareth.

"I-I was caught," she blubbered. "By the priest."

"You bloody fool!" Gareth growled, advancing toward her. "I told ye to run, didn't I?"

Shamed, Jessica looked at her feet, nodding.

"Yes, Pa."

"Serves you right for being so bloody daft." He raised a hand to smack her but she scurried back as Jake rose to put himself between the girl and Gareth.

"No 'arm done, Pa," Jake grumbled, casting Jessica a warning look.

"No one asked ya, boy!" The slap that had been intended for Jessica now landed on Jake's face but the boy did not flinch, fully accustomed to taking the brunt of Gareth's anger. Jessica swallowed a whimper, knowing her reaction would only anger Gareth more.

Erin extended her fingers toward the smaller girl, urging her closer but Jessica was transfixed by Gareth's reddening face. She backed away, sticking her hands in the depth of her pinafore until her back landed against the far wall.

"You didn't bring them here, did ye?" Gareth demanded. Jessica's hand closed around something in her pocket, eyes widening.

"No, Pa. I…I ran off the first chance I got."

"Stupid girl. I wonder why I bother with you at all. You left us to all the heavy lifting on our own so ye could sleep inside the church, it that right?"

She withdrew her hand and stared at the silver coin in her palm, eyes popping at the sight.

When did that get there?

Once more, she thought of the dreams and Mr Allen singing to her softly.

It hadn't been a dream! He put it in me pocket!

Gareth and Jake's eyes grew large at her find.

"What've you got there?" Gareth demanded, pushing Jake aside to close in on her. He snatched it out of her hand and peered intently.

"It's real, right?"

Jessica swallowed and shrugged.

"I don't know."

"It's real," Gareth concluded, slipping the piece into his own pocket. "Perhaps you aren't wholly useless after all."

He spun away to retreat to his section.

"Now, shut your holes, the lot of you. I'm right weary after last night—even if Jessie was able to sleep well."

He gave her a scathing look before stomping away and Jessica sank into Erin's waiting arms. Her pulse raced and she felt slightly sick again.

"Are you all right?" Erin murmured, searching her face. Jake shuffled closer.

"We were worried about ye, stupid. Why didn't ye run?"

"She was ill, you idiot," Erin barked sharply. "She didn't deign to get caught."

Jake offered Jessica a lopsided smile.

"Yes, I reckon that's true. Where did ye get that coin, Jessie? Did ye take it from one of the graves?"

Jessica shook her head, guilt blinding her.

"No…a priest…" she mumbled, not entirely clear on how it had come to be.

"Well, I never knew men of the cloth had so much extra coin t' spare!" He snorted contemptuously. "Perhaps we're taking from the wrong types."

"Hush your fat mouth," Erin growled. "Talking of robbing priests. Have you no shame at all?"

Jake was unfazed by Erin's indignation.

"Is it much different than taking from graves? They're on church land, sacred ground. It's apt to be less work if we steal from the living."

Jessica was aghast, his comparison accurate to her mind. What was the difference?

"You're spouting nonsense," Erin shot back at him. "Be grateful that Jessie is back and off you go."

He yawned and stretched. "I'm glad yer back, Jessie, but like Pa, I'm exhausted and tired of listening to Erin's squawking. Back to sleep I go."

Jessica snuggled down against Erin, her heart still racing.

"Are you all right?" Erin whispered again after Jake had reclaimed his spot on the hard floor. She wrapped her hole riddled blanket around Jessica and they lay down to stare at one another.

"Yes," Jessica reassured her.

"You're not feeling ill?"

Jessica shook her head.

"What happened? What did they do? Where did they take you?"

"T-they were very kind te me," she confessed. "I fainted and woke in a room in the dormitories. It had clean sheets and it smelled nice."

"I imagine so," Erin commented dryly. "Anywhere that don't reek of rubbish and mouse droppings is apt to be heaven."

Jessica's heart panged.

"They fed me and offered a bath," Jessica went on, recalling the details of her stay. It did not feel real now, on the dank, stinking ground next to Erin.

"Clearly you did not accept." Erin giggled. "Why not?"

Jessica pursed her lips.

"T'was a sin for me to be there in the first place," Jessica muttered. "They didn't know I was robbing graves."

Erin seemed taken aback by her response.

"The church is for everyone—even sinners."

Jessica could not abide by Erin's thinking.

Mr Allen and Father Thompson would never have permitted me to stay had they known the truth.

"You should have taken the bath," Erin said and tittered, but her eyes shadowed. "Or, then again, perhaps it's best that you did not come home clean. Gareth would have had something to say about it."

"I wish 'e 'adn't taken the coin," Jessica blurted out. Erin's black eyebrows shot up.

"You must have known he would when you showed it to him."

"I didn't know it was there," Jessica confessed. "Mr Allen must have snuck it into me pocket while I slept."

"He sounds kind," Erin said wistfully. She shrugged off her own reverie. "But you must realise that whatever we bring home goes into Gareth's palm."

"Yes, I know," Jessica agreed quickly. "I don't much mind the sharing but…"

She trailed off and shifted her eyes away, feeling foolish.

"But what?" Erin demanded impatiently.

"It's much like stealing from a priest, innit?"

Erin balked.

"No, it's not!" she fired back hotly. "The priest gave it to you and you gave it to Gareth. That's not stealing at all."

Jessica reasoned that Erin was technically correct but she could not shake the uneasy feeling in her gut.

"Now hush your mouth. I need another hour of sleep at least."

Erin turned on her side and Jessica wrapped a kind arm around her waist, snuggling closer to absorb her sister's heat.

This is me home, she thought, dismissing the previous fantasies she had permitted. *God doesn't watch us here.*

Despite her well-rested night, Jessica's eyes grew heavy, her breaths synching with Erin's.

She dreamt again about rosewater and lavender but the scent was intermingled with incense, spilling over the clean sheets of her church bed.

"I wish you hadn't left," Mr Allen murmured, setting down his bible to stare at her with caring green eyes. "God forgives you—provided you ask."

Jessica shook her head.

"No…not always."

"Yes, Jessica Joy. Always."

His face changed and the smell of lavender overtook all else, the woman's humming flooding Jessica's ears. Mr Allen was gone and the faceless angel from her dream returned to pour rosewater over her head.

Even then, Jessica knew she was dreaming but she secretly wished that she would never wake and live in that place forever.

CHAPTER 7

"Will we go back to that graveyard again tonight?"

Gareth lowered the flask in his hands, peering out toward the girl with rheumy eyes and a scowl.

"Have you taken full leave of your senses?" he yipped. "How many more signs from God Almighty do you require to see that we should not be there? We barely escaped by the skin of our teeth last night. There's no doubt that this time we'll be shot upon should we return."

Disappointment clouded Jessica's disposition and she pressed her lips together to keep from arguing.

"I'm surprised ye'd want te go back there," Jake added, following Gareth's harsh words. "Weren't ye captured?"

I'd 'ardly call it a capture, Jessica thought but wisely did not put a voice to her objection.

"Where will we hunt tonight then?" she asked instead.

"St. Alma's," Gareth announced, much to the chagrin of the children.

"We've already done that graveyard te death!" Jake complained, not noting his own pun. Erin tittered but Gareth's scathing look silenced her.

"I've other enterprises in the works," he snapped. "In the interim, you'll check for fresh graves. I've 'ad it on good authority that there are half a dozen new souls buried there today. Stagecoach disaster, as I heard it."

Jessica shuddered to think of such a wreckage.

"What other enterprises, Pa?" Erin asked, draping a protective arm over Jessica's neck.

"That's for me to know and you to find out," Gareth retorted. His face softened as he looked at Erin. "You'll have a rest today. I'll need you fresh with what's to come."

"No working the docks?" Erin asked hopefully. Jessica also despised the task of pickpocketing during daylight hours.

"Not today," Gareth replied, rising from his place against the stone wall. "Be ready for this eve. I'll return before then."

"Where are you going?" Erin demanded. Gareth's frown silenced her and her arm drew tighter around Jessica's body. Without responding, Gareth climbed over the crumbled walls, his walking stick in hand until he had disappeared from the view of the children.

"Why do I feel 'e's up te no good?" Jake muttered, more to himself than the girls. "It's never a good sign to see 'im 'working on enterprises.'"

"You recall the distillery?" Erin chuckled without mirth.

"'Ow could I forget? 'e wasted all the coin we collected on that operation," Jake grumbled. Jessica was too small to remember the details of that venture but her siblings had regaled her with the downfall of Gareth's business venture. Liam had been most incensed about the failure, his pickpocketing skills for naught when every penny had been squandered.

"I wonder how Liam is faring," Jessica muttered unexpectedly. Jake and Erin eyed her, their sardonic smiles fading.

"I 'aven't much 'eard from him. 'Ave ye?" Jake asked Erin. She scoffed.

"Did you think he would send a letter in the post?" she retorted sarcastically. "Or perhaps send a carrier pigeon? How could I have heard from him?"

"I think it's odd that—" Jake began.

"I think you're odd for asking stupid questions all the time," Erin cut him off. "Liam has finally achieved what was promised and you ruin it with your bitterness. That's quite enough."

She folded her arms under her tiny bosom and scowled at Jake.

"Come along, Jessica. We have a day with which to do as we please." She lowered her voice and dropped to Jessica's height. "And I may have a shilling or two for roasted hazelnuts."

Jessica's eyes bulged but Erin pressed her finger to her lips.

"Our secret, right? Don't go telling Pa about it." She straightened her body and turned to Jake, her grin evaporating. "You can come too if you'll stop being so miserable."

Jake shrugged and nodded, following as Erin led the way out of the shopfront and onto the street.

A light drizzle had commenced but the children barely noticed, giggling to one another as they found a hazelnut vendor near the port. The man eyed the scraggly children with thinly veiled contempt, demanding payment before producing a bag for them to share.

They wandered toward the river and Jessica remembered something.

"What did ye do with the body?" she asked. Erin stopped chewing long enough to shoot a look at Jake.

"Yes, Jake, what did you do with the body?" she repeated. Jake shifted his weight uncomfortably and shrugged his shoulders.

"I left it with Pa," he replied. "Not sure what he done with it."

Erin paled.

"Is it at the shop then?" she demanded. Jake shook his head, flakes of dirt flying over his face. His features were sharpening, the boy becoming a man almost overnight it seemed.

"I didn't smell it," he joked as Erin groaned, tossing a hazelnut toward him. Jake caught it in his mouth. "I don't know what Pa did with it."

Erin's eyes shadowed and she grew quiet as Jake jumped up on a boulder and began to make strange faces at Jessica. The girl giggled, enjoying her personal circus until Erin announced it was time to return to the shop.

"Already?" Jessica pouted. She had almost forgotten there was work to be done that night. Afternoon light struggled through the grey, low-hanging clouds and by now the children were soaked.

"Yes, now," Erin insisted, rising from her own rock. She brushed off her tattered skirts and together, they climbed off the banks toward the winding streets. Gareth was waiting for them on Elm Street, his face flushed.

"Where in God's name have you three been?" he barked. But his tone was less harsh than usual, his eyes bright and excited.

"You gave us a day, Pa," Erin reminded him.

"Yes, yes, come with me." He ushered them inside where the children paused.

"What's this now?" Jake demanded, eying the potato sacks. Mud oozed from the poor seals over the ground.

"This is our new endeavour," Gareth announced with pride. His declaration was met with blank stares.

"Potatoes?" Erin asked tentatively.

"No, you fool," he snickered. "Go. Pick one up."

Erin frowned and shook her head.

"They must weigh five stone a piece!" she protested.

"Yes," Gareth agreed gleefully. "Go on. Pick one up. Each of you."

Jessica slid forward, nervously watching her street siblings do the same. It felt like a trick to her and she could see that her companions had the same sense.

Jake reached for the first sack, grunting as he managed to lift it before dropping it unceremoniously at his feet.

"You'll improve with time," Gareth said confidently. "Erin. Your turn, girl. Pick one up."

"Pa, she cannot—"

Erin glowered Jake into silence and reached for a sack. Wincing, she half-managed to pull it into her arms but it fell almost instantly. Gareth frowned.

"You will need more practice. Jessie?"

"NO!" Jake and Erin spoke in unison.

"She's been ill, Pa, and she'll hurt herself," Erin added, stepping in front of Jessica.

"I want te try too!" Jessica protested, eager to show her own strength.

"You see? Jessie's got a better work ethic than both of you combined," Gareth snapped. "Step aside and let her show you how it's done."

"Jessie…" Jake muttered but she marched forward and grabbed for a sack. Panting and struggling, she barely stood it upright.

"Leave her be," Erin growled, pulling the girl back before she could damage her slight frame.

"You'll all need practice," Gareth announced, showing off his own power with one arm. He seized a mud-filled bag and lumped in under his arm, leering at the children with rotting teeth.

"Why?" Jake wanted to know. "What is this?"

"This is how we'll earn our coin going forward." Jake eyed him suspiciously but Gareth was not finished. "There will be no more robbing previously robbed graves. There will be no more scouring locations for new bodies and lost treasure."

The children held their collective breaths, barely able to believe his words.

"From today onward, we'll take the bodies and sell them to medical schools," he concluded, beaming wider than Jessica had ever seen him smile.

Stunned silence met his fevered statement.

"What!" Erin sputtered, the first of the three to recover. "Have you lost your wits?"

"Who in God's name would pay for rotting corpses?" Jake followed. Jessica was too shocked to speak at all.

Gareth's smile evaporated as he realised the others did not share in his excitement. He stomped his walking stick against the ground and spat.

"Fools! I should have known you dimwits would not appreciate the genius of this venture!" he hissed, throwing his hands up. The children recoiled, anticipating the blow which never came. "Medical schools are clamouring for cadavers and the uppity scholars who attend have no shortage of funds to disperse."

He reached into his pocket and withdrew a fistful of coins, causing the children to gasp.

"This is from yesterday's body alone," he said and chuckled when he saw their faces. "Think of how much more there is to come with three a night!"

"Jessie cannot possibly carry a body on 'er own!" Jake growled. "Nor can Erin for that matter."

"It's a horrid idea!" Erin squeaked, shaking her head. Her grey eyes stormed over. "How would we manage?"

"I'll not hear your collective whinging. You want for a beautiful life, don't ye?" Gareth rasped. "How do you think we come by it?"

Goosebumps rippled down Jessica's body as Gareth pointed toward the sacks again.

"Get to practicing," he growled. "I won't do without two corpses tonight."

He lowered his walking stick and strode off, leaving the children to gape at one another in horror.

∽

The first year was torturous, frozen winter grounds enhancing the woe of lifting and transporting the bodies from the cemeteries to the medical schools. Gareth eventually invested in a wheelbarrow but by the time Jessica was thirteen years old, she had muscles but no meat upon her bones. She sprouted taller but no wider.

Gareth's claims of riches did not come to fruition either. They were always "five more bodies" away from finding proper shelter or purchasing a real slab of meat. Jessica's feet grew hardened with callouses and the copied list of names she could not read grew larger on the page in her toe. Her heart hardened too, Gareth collecting two more children over the years to join their small family.

Annaleigh came a year later, a four-year-old who cried for her mother every night. Drake arrived the year after that—a quiet, mousy haired lad of five who barely spoke at all.

Erin tended to the children as she had Jessica but the younger girl could not find a bond with the newcomers. She was too tired to be a mother and Gareth did not expect it of her.

Yet for all her cynicism, not a day passed that Jessica did not close her eyes and put herself back in the bedroom of the church, under Mr Allen's kindly stare. Her dreams were filled with a mishmash of rosewater and heavy, wooden crosses.

While Gareth refused to return to St. Michael's churchyard again, Jessica sometimes stole into the area, hoping to get a glimpse of Father Thompson and Mr Allen once more.

She wondered if Mr Allen was now Father Allen.

"Jessie, will you play with me?"

The small, sweet voice forced Jessica's attention toward her feet where Annaleigh stared up at her with imploring blue eyes.

"Off te bed with ye," Jessica told her sternly. "We've work te do tonight and I won't hear yer whining that yer tired."

"Jessie!" Erin chided her with a stern look. "Come along, Anna. I'll sing to you. Would ye like that?"

Annaleigh brightened and she collected Drake to follow Erin back out of the alleyway. The shopfront on Elm Street had been purchased and men worked to restore the building to some of its previous glory, leaving Gareth's crew homeless again. They moved along the city, finding random shelters amongst awnings and barns but mostly, they were moved on back onto the street.

"We're five corpses from finding shelter, a real house with proper walls," Gareth had said again, just the previous night. "You'll have to do better with stripping the bodies for goods if ye want to eat."

He spoke to the little ones when he said this and they hung their heads in shame. Jessica and Erin had exchanged a cynical glance.

"Where in tarnation is that boy!" Gareth's voice echoed through the laneway and Jessica raised her head.

"Who?"

"Jake!"

"I'm here, Gareth."

Erin appeared at the far end of the alley, a little child on each hand as Jake showed his face. Jessica could not be sure when Jake had begun referring to Gareth by his first name but it had been ongoing for some time. At seventeen, he had become a strapping young man, certainly more man than boy now. Despite his poor diet, he had managed to fill out well about the shoulders and hips but he was nowhere as large as Gareth. The older man's face paled, eyes bugging to see Jake.

"W-what is that?" Gareth sputtered. Jessica's brow shot up at his tone. She had never heard him so flustered. Half turning, her eyes fell on what had upset Gareth so much.

A small boy in dirty pants and a torn cardigan stared, amazed at the people in the laneway. Jessica's heart twinged at the sight of his dark, inquisitive eyes, pudgy little hand curled around one of Jake's fingers.

"This 'ere is Matty," Jake announced. "He's going te live with us now."

Gareth scoffed but Jessica's heart lunged at the announcement.

"The hell he is!" Gareth barked. "That boy is no more than two."

"He is eighteen months and 'as nowhere to go," Jake insisted. "The little ones can watch over 'im."

Jessica lowered herself to the ground, eyes fixed on the little boy. Instantly, a smile curved over his lips, warming her chest.

"I won't have you bringing children here, willy-nilly!" Gareth spat.

"Why not? Ye do it without asking us!"

Gareth's face turned red and Jessica's breath caught. She glanced over her shoulder at Erin who balked at Jake's insolence.

"I bring lost souls together for their protection!" he growled, advancing on Jake. The young man did not falter but Jessica saw his hand tighten over Matty's.

"That is precisely what I've done," Jake insisted. "The boy needs a 'ome, a family. Will ye just throw 'im back on the street?"

"We are already on the streets!" Gareth countered. "We haven't a roof, in case you've failed to notice."

"Whose fault would that be, *Gareth*?"

Jessica could not smother the gasp before it fell from her lips but Gareth was far too incensed to hear it. He stormed closer, his fist raised toward Jake's defiant face.

"Pa, no!" Annaleigh howled.

Gareth froze as he realised all his children's eyes were upon him. Never had Jessica seen his face tinge such a shade of red before. Gareth did not look at the smaller children but he did lower his fists, much to Jessica's relief.

"I have my hands quite full without another mouth to feed!" Gareth snarled when he had found his voice. "If this boy stays, his meals will come from your portions."

Jake snorted.

"Then we'll both starve, right?"

Jessica silently willed Jake to be quiet, reading the rage in Gareth's eyes. But she suspected that Jake knew precisely what he was doing by rousing their guardian's ire. Matty whimpered as Gareth drew closer and the noise stopped the older man again.

"Ingrate, petulant, contemptible scallywag," Gareth hissed, shoving Jake aside to march away, his fury simmering behind him. Jessica released a breath and rose to her full height. Before she could utter a word, Erin leapt forward.

"You've gone and done it now," Erin rasped, rushing toward Jake.

"Ye say that every time," Jake reminded her dryly. Erin was not amused.

"Where in God's name did you find this one?"

Jake shook his head and turned to Matty but the boy had fixed his gaze on Jessica.

"This 'ere is Jessie and Erin. They're the two biggest and they'll look out for ye, right? That's Anna and Drake. Ye'll be good friends with them."

Matty continued to stare at Jessica with unblinking eyes as if no one else was around.

"He likes you, Jessie." Jake chuckled, releasing the boy's hand. Matty toddled forward. Again, Jessica crouched down, outstretching her arms to catch him from falling.

"Jake, where did you find him?" Erin demanded again. "Gareth isn't wrong. We do have too many mouths to feed."

Matty stumbled into Jessica's arms, and she swooped him up, unable to stop staring at his plump cheeks and button nose. He giggled, awed by Jessica's bright blue eyes.

"Does it much matter if there's one more?" Jake grumbled. "They hardly eat at his age."

"That's hardly the point," Erin insisted. "Eventually, he'll eat his weight in food. You should…"

Jessica tuned them out, stepping back with the little one in her arms to join the other children who cooed at their newest brother. Whatever danger Gareth had posed was gone for now and they were eager to study the baby's face.

"What's his name?" Annaleigh wanted to know.

"Matty," Jessica said.

"Can I hold him?"

"No," Jessica replied with far more harshness than she intended. Annaleigh's luminous blue eyes filled with tears and she felt a stab of guilt.

"Oh, all right," Jessica recanted. "But just for a moment."

She reluctantly thrust Matty into Annaleigh's arms. The child struggled with the weight of him against her own small frame.

"You best not drop 'im," Jessica told her warningly. "Jake'll be madder than 'ades if you do."

"I won't!" the little girl huffed, the effort of keeping him up too much for her. Matty began to cry, extending chubby fingers toward Jessica.

"Give 'im here," Jessica snapped, snatching the child back. Immediately, Matty calmed and Jake joined her side. Annaleigh was crestfallen, her lower lip trembling.

"It takes some practice te 'andle babies," Jake told the youngest girl softly to stop her from crying. "Albeit it seems that Jessie is a natural."

"Jessie don't like us none," Annaleigh sobbed. "She only likes babies!"

Erin quickly came to comfort the little girl but Jessica hardly noticed her upset. She was as transfixed by the child as she had been by the stone angel in St. Michael's graveyard.

This angel's real. I can touch his face anytime I want.

Jake gave her a tender smile but Jessica caught the expression of sadness attached. Her eyes narrowed slightly, her senses honing at the expression.

"Where's 'is mother?" Jessica asked pointedly, sensing more to the story than her urchin brother professed. Jake visibly swallowed, the bob of his Adam's apple grating over the scruff of his neck. He hesitated but realised that Jessica would not easily leave the subject alone.

"Gone," he answered simply. He paused and looked affectionately at the boy. "But perhaps ye'll 'elp with that, Jessie."

Again, Jessica fixed her eyes on the sweet, handsome face of the cherub-cheeked boy and nodded slowly.

"Right," she agreed. "I'll 'elp where I can."

CHAPTER 8

Jessica opened the page, wet and worn from years of travel and weather, straining to read the words again. She still did not know what they said but after hundreds of robbed graves, some of the numbers became familiar. She knew the twos and sixes, occasionally confusing them with nines.

"What've you got there?"

Erin's question caused Jessica to gasp and the page fluttered to the ground. Outside the abandoned house, rain drove in sheets against the wooden porch, sparks of lightning igniting the otherwise dim interior. Gareth only permitted two candles lit at a time and no lamps. He did not wish to waste the oil nor attract attention of passersby who knew the Killingers had passed from influenza only days earlier. Gareth had found out about the old couple's untimely demise through his man at the medical school, giving the family shelter for a few days but there was no reason for a light to be flickering in the house that was not occupied.

"Do you still carry that with you?" Erin chuckled, dropping down to pick up the discarded page. "After all these years?"

Jessica's eyes widened.

"Ye know what it is?"

"You're not as sly as you think you are, Jessica Joy." Jessica beamed with pleasure at the use of her 'surname.' She had been sprinkling it in conversations, hoping that her siblings and Gareth would use it. So far, only Erin had bothered. Jake thought her obsession with something so trivial was foolish and the others were too young to care one way or another. Gareth mocked her on occasion.

"What foolish surname is Joy?" he chortled. "Good heavens, girl. I thought you were too old for these childish fantasies. Should I find ye nappies, ye big baby?"

Erin eyed the page and sighed. "It's a pity we can't read."

"Is it though?" Jessica replied. "I think it's best we don't recall the names of those we've violated."

Erin cast her a sidelong look.

"And yet you continue to copy the headstones on this same, sodden piece of paper," Erin laughed. "Why do you do it?"

"Erin!"

Gareth's voice travelled down the stairs toward them. Instantly, Erin tensed, her face paling in the low light.

"I'll be there in a moment…Pa."

She physically shuddered to say the word and Jessica's smile faded also.

"Ye needn't go," Jessica told her urgently. "Tell him Drake needs yer or—"

"If I don't go now, he'll only demand later," Erin interjected. "It's best I get it out of the way."

Jessica exhaled, feeling bad for her companion but there was nothing she could do. Erin had accepted her fate with the same quiet indignity she had everything else.

"I wish it weren't so," Jessica muttered.

"He'll be calling on you soon enough," Erin told her, rising from the floor to endure Gareth's appetites. Jessica laughed dubiously.

"Me? 'ardly. Still sees me as a child."

Erin grimaced.

"You are hardly a child, Jessie. Have you bothered to look in a mirror lately?"

Both were young women now, Jessica at sixteen and Erin, twenty-one. Yet Jessica still regarded herself as the same spindly-legged girl who had fallen face-first into an open grave, despite the fact that she had become quite adept at the task of grave robbing.

Erin vanished into the house, leaving Jessica to wander through the building in search of a looking glass. Drake, Annaleigh, and Matty curled up at the hearth, a twine of legs and arms against a diminishing fire. Jessica paused and stared at the littlest boy.

How is 'e four already?

The past two and a half years had flown by in a blink of an eye. These days Matty clung to Jessica as if she were his real mother while Erin tended to the other children.

Matty stirred in his sleep and Jessica continued her search for a mirror which she found in the downstairs bedroom. Upstairs, groaning and creaking could be heard, causing Jessica's stomach to flip but she forced it out of her mind and fixed her eyes on the mirror.

A small gasp escaped her lips as she took in the bedraggled woman before her. Erin had not lied when she had said that she had matured over the years, a fact that had escaped Jessica's own attention.

The top part of her dress stretched over her top half, the torn sweaters doing little to hide her budding figure.

"Hey, 'ave ye gone vain in yer old age?" Jake teased, entering the house, dripping from head to toe.

Jessica turned to face him.

"Where've ye been?"

He waved a hand dismissively. "Is Matty asleep?"

Jessica nodded, searching for a blanket to dry him. A squeal from upstairs caused Jake to frown, his jaw twitching as his eyes traveled toward the stairs.

"Are they up there?"

Jessica nodded again.

"Bloody bastard," Jake muttered, stomping toward the front room where the children slept. Eager to take his mind off Erin and Gareth, Jessica rushed to his side.

"I think I might have me a bath tonight," she informed him. "Will ye 'elp me with the water?"

Jake's brow raised.

"Well, now, 'ave ye been invited te a royal gala with 'er Majesty?"

Jessica smiled enigmatically.

"No," she replied. "I thought I might go te church tomorrow."

~

"Come along, Matty," Jessica urged, half-dragging the boy along the damp streets. The rain had finally let up but a wheel from a carriage landed in a large puddle and splashed over their very best clothes as they headed toward St. Michael's Church.

Jessica's palms were sweaty, slipping out of Matty's several times as they drew closer to the building. She had not been inside since the day she had run off, seven years earlier and she found herself questioning her own decision.

It's 'igh time I thanked Father Thompson and Mr Allen...Father Allen...for what they did for me that day.

Erin's comment the previous night had sparked a desire deep inside Jessica. For years she had wanted to see the priests and offer her gratitude but not with them knowing who she was. Erin made her realise that Jessica did not look anything like the bony-legged girl who had stolen away at the crack of dawn. The men would not recognise her, and she could give her thanks without them being any the wiser.

"Matty, stop with yer splashing!" Jessica reprimanded the boy. He grinned at her sheepishly and stomped his foot in another puddle, covering Jessica's worn but pretty blue dress. She could not be cross with his impish smile, his face already caked in dirt despite the washing she had given him that morning.

"Hurry back," Gareth growled when Jessica had told him where they were going. "There's too much for Erin to do on her own."

Jessica promised she would return after services but she did not inform Gareth where she intended to go. He would not understand her need to free her heavy soul of the burdens which she continued to lay upon it. Seeing the priests and offering her gratitude was Jessica's own small way of asking for God's forgiveness.

The stone building loomed in front of her as it had in her dreams and nightmares so many times before. She paused to take it in, eyes darting toward the stone angel. He was still there, his finger gesturing her forward.

"Are we gonna talk te God, Jessie?" Matty asked.

"Yes, me darling, we are," Jessica replied, inhaling. She closed her fingers more tightly around Matty's and gently yanked him forward. Matty's eyes widened as they entered, taking in the high ceilings and stained glass.

He untangled his hand from hers and Jessica whispered after him.

"Stay close, Matty. Don't venture off now."

She slid into the closest pew, realising too late that the morning services had already concluded. But that seemed unimportant as her eyes rested on two familiar faces, gathering their belongings from the apse.

Is that Mr Allen?

It was difficult to believe that the dashing young man, chatting pleasantly with a much-aged Father Thompson was the same one she had thought about for years.

"I daresay, Father, she has been giving you quite a look all through service." Father Allen chuckled, his voice low and gentle, just as she remembered it. He was undoubtedly the man she had come to see.

Father Thompson turned his white head toward a middle-aged woman, stripping the cloths from the altar, oblivious to their teasing but she did raise her head more than once to beam widely at the older priest.

"If I were an older man, I would vie for her attention myself," Father Allen joked. Jessica giggled before she could stop herself. Immediately, she clamped her hand over her mouth, looking away too late.

"Oh? Who's there?" Father Allen called out, his eyes locking on Jessica. She balked, unable to move as he and Father Thompson moved toward her. Hastily, she rose, smoothing out her skirt which was now splayed with mud from Matty's adventures.

"I—apologies, Father, uh, Fathers," Jessica blubbered, feeling her cheeks flush crimson. The plan, so well-rehearsed in her mind blew away like sand in the wind.

"Do I know you?" Father Allen asked, his brow furrowed as he neared. Jessica shook her head and turned her face away.

No, 'e cannot remember me. It's been too long and 'e wouldn't 'ave thought of me anyway.

Yet the way his eyes bored into her gave Jessica's stomach an anxious lurch. Father Thompson showed no indication of recognition as he extended his hand.

"We are always welcoming of new congregants to St. Michael's, my dear. What is your name?"

Jessica lifted her fingers to touch hands with Father Thompson but as she did, she realised how poorly she had cleaned under her nails. The dim light by the bath had done little to clean the crevices that had been sorely neglected over the years. Instantly, she snatched her hand back, breaths escaping in short, uneasy rasps.

"Oh my word!"

The excited squeal of a woman turned all attention toward the pulpit. Jessica's eyes bugged as she realised Matty had found the altar.

"It appears that Mrs Barlow has found your son," Father Thompson chuckled, a twinkle of affection touching his eyes. Jessica leapt to her feet and rushed toward the pair.

"You needn't worry, Madam. Mrs Barlow has grandchildren of her own. She's quite harmless," Father Allen called out after her but Jessica barely heard his reassurances.

Panting, she joined Matty and the woman at the pulpit. Mrs Barlow cooed over Matty, stroking his wayward curls and the boy accepted the doting attention with pleasure.

"Isn't he a darling, Fathers?" she called back to them. "I'd like nothing more than to bring him home and give him a bath."

She beamed at Jessica who paled at her words.

"Here you are, my love," Mrs Barlow went on, producing a ripe apple from somewhere Jessica could not see. Eagerly,

Matty reached for it, grinning happily. "Oh, he's just a darling. What's his name?"

Panic flooded Jessica's gut, the idea of a stranger taking Matty filling her with sickness.

I shouldn't 'ave brought 'im here. I shouldn't 'ave come 'ere at all! Now I'll lose Matty for it!

"Are you all right? You're quite waxen—oh!"

Jessica snatched up Matty and ran toward the front doors, feeling the shocked looks at her back.

"Miss! Miss, are you all right?" Father Thompson demanded as she rushed past.

"Jessie, I want te stay with the nice lady!" Matty mumbled, his mouth full of apple.

She did not stop, her feet sinking into the wet mud along the graveyard. A dozen memories flooded her mind with every step, her eyes honed to the ground for open graves.

"Jessica!" Father Allen yelled from behind her. "Jessica Joy!"

She froze, if only for half a second, casting a glance behind her as Father Allen ran toward her. In her mind's eye, she was nine years old again and in his hand, he held a pistol.

Inhaling, she urged her legs forward, sprinting toward the street with Matty struggling in her arms the whole way.

"I reckon the lady 'as cake," Matty mumbled grouchily. Jessica did not loosen her grip on the boy, ducking down alleyways and through market streets until she was certain Father Allen was no longer on her heels.

Feeling as though her lungs were going to burst, Jessica collapsed against a stone wall, still clinging to Matty's hand.

He peered up at her with wide, brown eyes.

"Are ye dying, Jessie?" he asked plaintively. Jessica laughed and shook her head.

"No, not yet, me darling."

Matty took another bite of his apple and turned his head back toward the market, waiting patiently for Jessica to collect herself.

Slowly, her breathing returned to normal, and Jessica allowed herself to feel regret and shame for what she had just done.

Yet there was something else, another sensation creeping into her soul.

He remembered me. He remembered the name 'e gave me, too.

A smile quirked at the corners of her mouth and Jessica righted herself.

"Are ye all done then?" Matty asked, taking another bite of his apple.

"Yes. Let's go home?"

"We don't 'ave a home," Matty replied sensibly.

"No, we don't," Jessica agreed. "But we 'ave each other and that's seen us through some'ow."

Matty curled his small hand into Jessica's, and she exhaled a whoosh of breath, realising just how close she had come to losing him.

I'll never do that again, she vowed. *I'll forget about Father Allen. The past ought te lay where it is.*

CHAPTER 9

*J*essica's breathing had hardly regained regularity by the time she and Matty appeared at the Killinger house. Sunshine was attempting to break through the heavy clouds, fighting for a chance to be seen.

The weather mimicked the turmoil inside Jessica, a ray of hope threatening to venture through the darkness of panic and concern.

He recognised me! 'E's thought of me!

She found herself smiling now that the danger posed had been escaped. Henry Allen had indeed become an attractive man in the past seven years. Yet, had his eyes become kinder? The more she considered her actions of fleeing, the sillier she felt. He had meant her no harm and Matty's grin told Jessica that he had enjoyed his time in the church.

Sneaking through the garden gate as to not arouse the suspicion of neighbours, Jessica pulled Matty toward the back door and entered through the kitchen.

THE LITTLE STONE ANGEL 93

Loud voices radiated toward her, Gareth's overtaking them all.

"What in tarnation is 'appening 'ere?" Jessica demanded, releasing Matty's hand. Erin and the younger children cowered as Gareth stomped through the salon, smashing anything in his wake.

Gareth fixed his eyes on Jessica, baring his fetid teeth.

"And where in bloody hell have you been?" he hissed, rushing toward her. Protectively, Jessica stepped back, arms extended protectively over Matty. Unblinking, she met Gareth's eyes, noting streaks of red over his high-collar shirt.

"I told ye already. We went te church," Jessica shot back defiantly. The near-madness in her guardian's eyes caused her to balk. "What is all the fuss about?"

Gareth's gaze fixed on Matty's. He snatched the half-eaten apple from the boy's hand, causing Matty to squeak in protest.

"From where did this hail?" Gareth spat, suspicion clouding his face.

"The nice lady at the church," Matty explained earnestly, his chin quivering in fear. Like the other children, he was no stranger to Gareth's rages but Jake and Jessica did their best to protect him.

"What lady? What church?" Gareth fired out, advancing on Jessica. "Where did ye go, girl?"

"Pa, yer behaving poorly!" Jessica gasped, not understanding his anger. "What's happened?"

"Jake…" Erin whispered, forcing Jessica's head to whip around. She stared warily at her sister before scanning the room for signs of Jake.

"Where is 'e?"

If possible, Gareth's face stained a deeper shade of blue and a spastic cough erupted from his lungs, spraying them all with spittle. Jessica drew back, confusion fully encompassing her.

"Erin…?" she murmured under the sound of Gareth's hacking. He hovered over his walking stick, doubled over until Jessica was forced to close in upon him to ensure he was not dying.

"Pa are ye—" She was not permitted the opportunity to conclude her sentence as Gareth's cane lashed out to smack her against the knees. Jessica's legs buckled and she fell forward as Gareth garnered his composure.

"Pa!" Erin cried out, rushing to Jessica's side. "She only meant to help!"

Annaleigh mewled, her large eyes flooding with tears.

"Stop your snivelling or I'll give you something to snivel about!" Gareth roared to the girl. Immediately, Annaleigh clamped her rosebud lips closed and cowered back as Drake draped an arm over her, the two striving to disappear into the shadows.

Jessica righted herself, willing away the tears of humiliation which sprang into her eyes.

"Nothing but trouble, the lot of you!" he thundered, slamming the end of his cane against the ground. Again, Annaleigh whimpered and Jessica threw herself between the enraged man and the little girl.

"Please, Pa, tell me what's 'appened," she begged, watching her tone. "Per'aps I can 'elp."

Gareth scoffed, another cough falling from his lips but to Jessica's relief, he spun away.

"You're just as useless as that thieving bastard, Jake," he rasped. Jessica's eyes widened and she glanced at Erin once more. For the first time, the younger woman noticed how pale her sister had grown.

"What of 'im?" Jessica pressed. "What did Jake do?"

"I should've know better than to trust a lowly urchin," Gareth huffed, his response answering nothing.

"He done stole from Pa," Drake piped up. Jessica whirled around to look at the usually silent child. Drake stood amongst shards of glass, his dark eyes frightened.

"He what?"

"You heard right, girl," Gareth growled. "He went off and started his own business, using our wares for his own benefit."

Jessica's mouth gaped.

"No…no, Jake wouldn't do something like that, Pa!" she protested. "Where is 'e? Ye must've misunderstood."

Gareth slapped her face.

"Are ye questioning me, girl?" he hissed. "He's gone. Run off like the thief in the night that he is."

Jessica rubbed at her cheek but continued to shake her head stubbornly.

"No, Pa," she insisted, "'e wouldn't."

Her eyes trailed toward Matty who began to cry, flopping down on the mess that Gareth had created in his rage.

He wouldn't leave Matty, 'e loves that bairn te much.

Jessica had long suspected that the bond between Jake and Matty extended circumstance and existed from blood. Over the years, she had watched the young man and boy grow close in ways she had only imagined between father and son. Even if Matty were not who Jessica believed him to be, she was adamant that Jake would never leave him behind.

"Jessie…" Erin whispered but it was too late for Jessica to protect herself from Gareth's wrath. His fist pummelled into her face.

"Is that where you've been all day?" he spat between blows. "Off consorting with that ruffian bastard?"

Jessica tasted blood in her mouth, raising her arms to ward off more of his blows. Yet she did not relent in her conviction.

"No, Pa!" she rasped, another punch landing on her. "Yer wrong about Jake. Ye know he would never leave Matty or us!"

"Stupid, insolent girl!" Gareth fumed, yanking her upright by her freshly cleaned hair, fistfuls of red tangled in his fingers as he dragged her toward the staircase. "I'll show you some respect!"

Dread consumed Jessica as she abruptly realised what Gareth intended to do. Erin's warning from the previous night flooded her mind and she struggled against him.

"No, Pa! Stop!" she cried. Erin rushed forward, yanking on Jessica's arm.

"No, Pa! Take me instead!" she choked, her face ashen with fear. "Leave her be. She's still a girl!"

Sick rose in Jessica's gut as Gareth's heavy boot shot out to kick at Erin, knocking the woman back into her horrified charges. Annaleigh screamed and Matty wailed, his cries echoing through the small, stone house.

"Shut them up before I do!" Gareth roared, jerking a flailing Jessica up the stairs. She fought ruthlessly against him, shoes catching on the steps but her efforts were futile against Gareth's brute strength.

"It's high time you learnt to respect me as the head of this family," Gareth rasped, ripping harder at her locks to throw her onto the landing atop the stairs. Below, the children watched the terrible scene unfold, their haunted eyes disturbing Jessica more than Gareth's violence.

"Stop!" she screamed again as he bore his weight down upon her, tearing at the hem of her dress. Bucking and scratching, she managed to shove him aside long enough to roll away from the stares of the children.

"Get back here, trollop," Gareth snarled, reaching the edge of her skirts. Jessica scrambled away, the fabric tearing in his hand but before she could take a step, Gareth threw his full weight against her, knocking Jessica back to the ground.

"Fighting will only make it worse."

Jessica squeezed her eyes shut as Gareth grunted, fumbling with his belt as she lay pinned beneath him. For all she had endured in her young life, she had never felt this level of terror. The man she had called "father" for all of her life was determined to take her in ways meant only for the holy union of marriage.

She found herself thinking of Erin and how many times her sister had endured the same terror at his hands. Fat tears rolled down her cheeks, Gareth Winston's true character showing with blinding clarity.

'It's true, 'e never saw us as anything but disposable children. We are nothing to 'im!

Her lids parted as Gareth struggled out of his trousers and again her eyes fell on the red streaks on his shirt.

Blood. That's flipping blood!

She had certainly seen enough of it in her time. The question was, whose blood was it?

A whisper in her mind asked where Jake had gone and Liam too. How had no one heard from any of the boys who had been promised "a beautiful life" by Gareth?

There never was "a beautiful life" for the boys on a farm. What has this evil monster done te my brothers!

A dozen images flashed through Jessica's mind, time slowing and racing simultaneously as Gareth forced her legs apart. Matty's wide, haunted eyes, Jake's bruised face, Erin's perpetual stare of brokenness. She could hear Annaleigh's sobs and Drake's whimpers.

She saw herself as a little girl, cowering in a grave as Gareth barked at her to shut up, poking at her with his dreaded walking stick.

The memory of coin wasted on whiskey and wine as the children starved, left to run amok barefoot. Gareth chewing bread while scolding the others that they would not eat due to their lack of work ethic.

From somewhere inside her, Jessica's own sense of rage erupted and when Gareth turned his head back toward her, leering hideously, she reacted. Her teeth gnashed into his cheek, pulling with unyielding ferocity until she pulled the skin from his face. Shock ignited his face, his body freezing atop her until she released the flap of flesh and went for his nose.

Howling, Gareth fell back, a filthy hand falling to his face as his pants fell around his ankles.

"You whore!" he bellowed. "They'll be hell to pay for this!"

In his bleeding and exposed state, Gareth inadvertently allowed her the chance to escape. Jessica wasted no time with this opportunity, her flapping shoes flopping down the stairs. He reached out to snatch her back but she had anticipated his move, sidestepping his red-stained hands.

The children gasped in horror to see her bustling down the steps but Jessica paid them no mind, yanking open the front door without any qualms about who might see them squatting on the Killingers property.

"JESSIE!" Erin yelled out after her but Jessica did not stop. The texture of Gareth's skin in her teeth made her gag but she could not stop to spit nor vomit. She had no doubt that if she slowed down for one moment, Gareth would catch her and force her into the same fate as her urchin brothers before her.

CHAPTER 10

Unshed tears blurred her vision, her footsteps racing through the winding, complicated laneways until Jessica did not know which way was which. She did not care for she headed away from the Killinger house and that was all that mattered.

"Good lord, Miss!" a dockworker cried, extending a finger to point at her face. "Are you injured?"

Jessica spared no response, her legs cramping as she continued through the stinking piers, hoping to meld with the crowd. In her haste to escape, she fumbled over the hem of her torn dress, stumbling headlong into an apple cart.

"Watch yer bloody way!" the vendor cursed her, eyes widening when he caught sight of the dishevelled, half-hysterical woman. "'Ave ye slaughtered someone then?"

Panic resurfaced in Jessica's gut as the man yelled out.

"Fetch a constable, now? I reckon the lass' done in 'er rib."

Gasping, Jessica spun to rush in the other direction, crashing into a smartly dressed gentleman who had no business in that part of town.

"Good heavens, Miss, are you mad?" he demanded, turning up his nose. "Someone send for a policeman at once! This woman is hysterical!"

The tears flowed now, freely down her cheeks to stain them with a fusion of blood and grime. She backed away, eyes fixed on the gentleman and vendor, lest the policeman surprise her.

"That'll do now." A calm, warm hand closed around Jessica's upper arm and she struggled to free herself as she spun around.

"I didn't murder anyone!" Jessica moaned, struggling against the woman. "Leave me be!"

"Hush, dear," she murmured. "I am a friend in God. Do you remember me?"

Hastily, Jessica blinked away her tears, wiping at her face as she looked about for the inevitable constable. There was no sign of a bobby but that did not mean one would not soon appear.

"Come along, Miss Joy," the woman murmured, forcing Jessica to stare fully at her kind rescuer for the first time.

"Mrs Barlow!" she gasped. The older woman smiled, her bright eyes gleaming as she nodded.

"So you do recall who I am," she said sweetly. "That makes for a less awkward conversation."

Dumbfounded, Jessica could do nothing but stare. Mrs Barlow did not lose her smile nor her patience.

"My house is just this way, dearie. Let's see you there, shall we?"

Jessica started to shake her head but the older woman held firmly to her, half-shoving her along the dockside.

"Or if you prefer, you could sit and await the constabulary, although I suspect their accommodations are not quite as pleasant as mine."

Swallowing, Jessica allowed the woman to guide her away from the water and up through several small backstreets where the crowds were much diminished. It was only then that Jessica realised how close she was to St. Michael's church.

"It *is* Miss Joy, isn't it?" Mrs Barlow asked kindly. "I fear I only heard Father Allen call after you and did not formally introduce myself."

"Jessica," she muttered. "Jessica Joy."

"A lovely name for a lovely young lady," Mrs Barlow chirped, leading the way over the cobblestone streets toward a small, charming house across the way. The steeple of St. Michael's was visible from the gate of the white picket fence but Jessica did not have time to relish in the sight of it.

"I am Mrs Penelope Barlow," the woman prattled on, securing the door behind her. "Although I see you've already gleaned as much."

Her cottage smelled of rosemary and onions, the scent oddly comforting to Jessica as she took in the charming surroundings and simple furnishings. In many ways it reminded Jessica of the Killinger house but never had she breathed easily inside those walls, knowing that at any moment, they would be thrust back into the cold, unforgiving streets.

Mrs Barlow nodded for her to sit at the wooden table in the kitchen before busying herself with firewood for the stove.

"It'll be warm in no time at all," she reassured Jessica who sat stiffly at the edge of her chair. It was already plenty warm enough to the girl, who had spent her life sleeping on icy grounds with rocks for beds, but she did not complain about the added heat.

"Will you tell me, are you injured?" Mrs Barlow asked, placing a kettle on top of the stove. Slowly, the terrified haze that had followed Jessica from Gareth's clutches began to diminish.

"No…" she mumbled, realising how she must look. "The blood isn't mine."

"Praise our Lord for small favours," Mrs Barlow said and sighed, her smile returning as she took a seat across from Jessica. "And the bairn?"

A newfound panic overcame Jessica as the realisation of what she had done settled in.

I've left Matty and the others with that brute! Poor Erin!

She jumped up, startling Mrs Barlow.

"Matty!" Jessica gasped. "I must return for me brother!"

Mrs Barlow's brow furrowed, and she shook her head.

"If you'll forgive my boldness, Miss Joy, I daresay you are in no position to go anywhere. You narrowly missed having yourself arrested at the docks and venturing out as you are will no doubt yield similar results."

The truth of her statement struck Jessica but she could not abide by the idea of leaving her street siblings in the hands of Gareth.

"I-I'll be careful on me return," Jessica sputtered. Yet even as she spoke the words, she wondered how she would manage. Gareth would be waiting for her and she could not take Matty under his watch. Even if she were able to steal Matty away, what of the others and where would they go that Gareth would not find them?

Slowly, Jessica sank back into her chair, her gut flipping with sorrow.

"You cannot help anyone before you help yourself, Miss Joy," Mrs Barlow told her firmly. "Whatever has become of you these past few hours, you're in no place to assist your brother."

Jessica clamped her lips together as Mrs Barlow rose to fetch a pot of tea. She wanted to blurt out the whole sordid tale and beg the genteel older woman about what was best to do but she dared not. Despite the odd coincidence that yet another from St. Michael's church had been there to save her, Jessica did not permit herself to lower her well armoured guard.

"Have a spot of tea," Mrs Barlow encouraged, pouring a steaming cup for the girl before returning the kettle to the stove. "I'll see about a bath for you."

Jessica spluttered the sip that had been in her mouth, spraying the liquid about the hard wood of Mrs Barlow's table.

"Oh, I couldn't—" she started to say but Mrs Barlow crisply cut her off.

"Again, if you will forgive me, Miss Joy, you are affright to behold. While I am deeply relieved that you are not hurt, I must confess that seeing you caked in another's blood is a concept considerably more daunting. For my sake, please accept my offering."

Jessica flushed and stared down at the cup before her.

"Very well," Mrs Barlow smiled again. "Sit tight and I'll return forthwith."

She disappeared into the tiny house, leaving Jessica to ferment over her tea.

I should go right now, she thought but made no move to rise from her chair. In her mind's eye, she saw Matty, reaching out for her with little, pudgy fingers, urging her to pick him up.

I'll go back for 'im at least. Jake would want me to care for 'im.

She recalled the terrible notions she'd had, crushed beneath Gareth's body and shuddered.

Has 'e done something to the lads? Are they dead?

"Come along, Miss Joy," Mrs Barlow sang, reappearing in the kitchen. "I've filled the tub with nice clean water. If you please?"

Jessica rose and followed her into the next room, gawping slightly to realise she had precisely done that. An old, metal tub steamed with water, presumably warmed by the fireplace nearby.

"Oh…" Jessica murmured. "I—thank ye, Mrs Barlow."

The words were foreign to her lips. She could not recall the last time she had shown gratitude to anyone.

"I'll leave you in peace, dear, but I did manage to find a dress from my younger days. It's hardly high fashion but there are not any tears or rips." She nodded toward a garment placed against the dining table. A lace collar and satin sash stole Jessica's breath. "I daresay the blue will be fetching with your eyes."

Mrs Barlow disappeared, securing the doors as she vanished, and Jessica slowly stripped down to lower herself into the water. The temperature was warmer than tepid and the flow seeped into every crevice of her battered body, easing the pain she had not realised she felt.

A pumice stone sat on the edge of the tub with a piece of lye soap. Jessica wasted no time scrubbing any reminder of Gareth off her body. When she had finished, the water was stained with filth but Jessica's long, red tresses curled upwardly around her bosom.

Mrs Barlow's dress fit snugly about Jessica's slender frame, indication that perhaps the older woman had at one time been much smaller. It was the finest dress Jessica had ever worn and she could not help but whirl about the room, feeling the swish of lace against her ankles. Her dancing was abruptly cut short when the sound of a man's voice muffled through the walls.

Her blood ran cold when Mrs Barlow knocked on the door.

"Miss Joy? You have a visitor, if you're so inclined to receive him."

Jessica's heart leapt to her throat.

"Miss Joy?"

"I—who is it?" she barked back. Mrs Barlow chuckled.

"I believe you'll know him when you see him," she replied lightly. Jessica's pulse raced in her veins and she crept toward the double doors. Beads of sweat formed at her brow.

Could Gareth 'ave found me? But 'ow?

Pressing her ear to the door, she listened.

"...God watching over her, Mrs Barlow," a low but warmly familiar voice murmured. "You truly are an angel."

Jessica threw open the door and gaped at Father Allen, her cheeks staining pink.

"Mr—Father Allen!" she breathed. Relief and joy coloured his comely face and he rose from his chair to greet her, smiling appreciatively as she neared.

"I daresay, that dress suits you much better than it ever did me," Mrs Barlow clucked. "I'll see if I cannot find more in that trunk for you. I certainly have no use for them after birthing five bairns."

"Oh ye needn't—" Jessica began to protest.

"Nonsense," Mrs Barlow interjected. "I had sought an excuse to leave politely and now I have it. I'll see about boots, too. I venture your feet are slightly smaller than mine."

Jessica was speechless at her kindness, but Mrs Barlow did not require a response. She beamed at the pair and vanished up the stairs, leaving the priest to study Jessica with happy eyes.

"How did ye know I was 'ere?" she asked, slowly lowering her body into a chair. Father Allen also took a seat, smiling.

"Mrs Barlow is something of a sly fox," he admitted. "She sent a message through a neighbour's boy."

"When?" Jessica asked, awed. The woman had barely been out of view.

"As I said, a sly fox!" He laughed. His face softened and he leaned across the table to touch her hand.

"I feel blessed to have the opportunity to see you again, Miss Jessica Joy. I've thought of you often over the years and I see now that I have worried for naught. You've become a lovely young lady with a child of her own."

Jessica balked and pulled her hand away, lowering her eyes.

He believes I've done well for myself. He has no idea of the truth.

Through her peripheral vision, she saw his expression of confusion.

"What is it?" he asked gently. "Why do you look so shamed?"

"Matty is not me child," she muttered breathlessly. "And I 'aven't done well in the least."

If he were surprised by her confession, he made no show of it, a pensive, understanding shadow befalling his eyes.

"Is that why you ran from me today?" he asked softly. "And why you ran all those years ago?"

A lump formed in Jessica's throat and she blinked several times to keep from crying but under Henry Allen's compassionate stare, she was powerless to stop the flow of words that had longed to spring from her mouth.

"I'm not good, Father," she whispered, brushing aside a stray tear. "I'm not worthy of yer kindness."

"I find that difficult to believe," he replied. She threw her head back and met his eyes squarely.

"I wasn't some lost, wandering soul ye found that night. Me family, we robbed graves, stealing from the dead and later even taking their bodies te sell."

Once again, Father Allen's face registered no surprise.

"Your family?" he repeated. "Tell me of them."

Jessica snorted and used her hands to wipe at her face but Father Allen produced a handkerchief for her. For a long moment, Jessica merely stared at it. She had never before been offered one.

"It will absorb better than your skin," he remarked teasingly. Pursing her lips, Jessica snatched it and dabbed at her cheeks.

"They aren't me real family, not by blood. Pa—Gareth—he found the lot of us and took us in over the years. We were made te steal and take te keep us in his good graces."

Father Allen's face hardened but he made no comment as Jessica went on.

"Jake and Erin and me, we lived alone awhile after Liam left. Then Pa found two more wee 'uns and brought them along. And Jake brought us Matty. I daresay the boy is 'is though."

"You care for them a great deal, don't you?"

Jessica sniffled and nodded, ashamed to meet his eyes.

"It's no excuse for the 'arm I've done," Jessica murmured. "God 'imself wouldn't 'ave time to pardon all me sins."

"Do you know who St. Michael is?" Father Allen said, the shift of topic catching her off guard.

"He's the man on yer church, isn't 'e?"

Father Allen chuckled.

"Yes. The church is named for him. He is an archangel, one of God's holiest warriors against evil. He's often depicted with a sword for his fighting knew no boundaries. God is a peaceful and loving God, but He realises that not all can be solved with simple answers."

Jessica stared at him blankly and Father Allen again reached for her hands. This time she did not pull away as he stared into her eyes.

"In all things good, there is some darkness," he explained. "And sometimes that darkness can work for good."

Jessica blinked again. A small smile quirked at the corners of his full lips and Jessica found herself transfixed by his mouth.

"You cared for your street siblings, did you not? Took care of them when they were ill, held them when they longed for their mothers?"

Jessica grimaced.

"I tried te. Erin was much better at it than me."

"You certainly care for Matty. I saw the way that boy regarded you. Like you were his own mother."

The compliment filled Jessica's heart.

"You did what was necessary to care for your family, Jessica," he concluded. "Perhaps not always the right way but your heart was not filled with evil intentions. You know what you did was wrong but it was without choice. Now that you are a grown woman, you must think to the future you wish for and find another means of supporting yourself—if you truly are repentant."

Jessica swallowed and studied his face with wide eyes.

"I am!" she breathed, wondering if it could truly be so simple. "Ye believe that my soul can be redeemed?"

"I'm certain of it."

They shared a private smile and Jessica flushed, gazing away again.

"Why 'ave you become a priest?" she blurted out before she could stop herself. Her blush deepened but Father Allen was not fazed by her question.

"Some claim they have always heard the calling of God but that was not me," he admitted. Jessica's eyebrows raised.

"The simple truth of it was that I once witnessed such an astounding act of kindness by a man and his wife, I could not imagine a life not helping those most in need."

Curiously, Jessica tipped her head.

"What did ye see?"

"There was a large, lumbering man who lived by the bridge near the Greenland Docks. Terrifying to most respectable folk who ventured in those parts but not to this young couple who took it upon themselves every day to walk past and offer him coin or bread. One day, he was simply not there anymore and when I asked about him, fearing he had passed, I was told this couple saw him home to sleep in their coach house and work for room and board."

"That man sounds like what Gareth looks like," Jessica muttered, not commenting on the stupidity of such an action. The event had changed Father Allen's life and she did not wish to diminish the passion in his heart.

"Does he?" Father Allen murmured. Jessica's eyes narrowed slightly, sensing he had something on his mind.

"What is it, Father?"

He smiled.

"I was thinking that perhaps there is a way to learn of your real family. The clergy has access to the baptisms in the area. Perhaps yours is listed."

"Assuming I was baptised at all," Jessica muttered sullenly.

"I feel that you have Christ in you, Jessica and it comes from somewhere."

"There's no sense in looking, Father Allen." She sighed. "I was left for dead with nary a scrap o' cloth to me body."

"Yes, but you did not fall from the sky, child. There's no harm in looking, is there?"

A peculiar sensation slithered down her spine and suddenly, Jessica realised it was hope.

All this talk of me fake family. My real family needs me. I shouldn't have stayed 'ere so long.

"I must find me brothers and sisters," she muttered, rising as though she were attached to a spring. Disappointment clouded his face.

"Please, stay a while longer," he pleaded as Mrs Barlow returned to the kitchen. She appeared equally surprised by Jessica's urge to leave.

"Thank you for yer 'elp—and guidance," she told the pair earnestly. "I promise I won't stay away this time. I'll return yer dress, Mrs Barlow."

"Heavens no." Mrs Barlow chuckled. "But do return soon. I'll bake scones for your arrival."

Jessica turned and rushed out of the house before Father Allen's imploring look could keep her in place.

"I daresay, Father Allen, those are stars in your eyes?" Mrs Barlow cawed as Jessica slipped out the back door. Her smile faded as the streets of East London appeared. Gone was the fleeting security she had known in Mrs Barlow's house. Gareth would be a force of terror when she arrived.

CHAPTER 11

"Lookie at the uppity wench!" Charles yodelled from his place among the crates. "Eddie, de ye see what I see?"

"Hells bells, is that lil Jessie?"

"She isn't so lil anymore, is she?"

The two displaced men cackled, exposing their missing teeth as Jessica slowed her gait to cast them a worried smile. The pair were brothers and landmarks in the neighbourhood, harmless as kittens the both.

"Where ye often lookin' so fancy, Miss Jessica?" Edward asked, thrusting aside his moth-eaten blanket. A putrid smell emanated from him, made all the worse against Jessica's freshly-washed skin. "I daresay, ye look like a right, proper lady!"

"What would ye know about proper ladies?" she teased them, her mind still fixed on what she might find at the Killinger house. Charles hooted and slapped his leg, a coughing fit erupting to commingle with his laughter.

"Out de way," a vendor grumbled, pushing his apple cart past Jessica. It was the very same man she had crashed into not three hours earlier. He straightened himself to see the attractive young lady, offering her a leering smile.

"Apple fer ye, Miss?"

Jessica eyed him dubiously, realising that he did not recognise her.

"No," she replied, secretly pleased at the inadvertent compliment. His grin faded and he marched on, his wheelbarrow in tow.

"Yer wee 'un's about," Charles quipped, straightening himself. "Lookin' right sad, he did."

Jessica tensed, her eyes narrowing.

"Come again?"

"The boy, Marcus?" Edward chimed.

"Matty, ye daft sard," Charles corrected him. Jessica balked, leaning closer to the vagabonds.

"He was 'ere?" she demanded, her head whipping from side to side as if to locate any sign of the boy. It was still quite a distance to the Killinger house. "Where did ye last see 'im?"

"Over yonder, me thinks." Even from where she stood, Jessica was overpowered by the reek of rancid whiskey radiating from the man.

"Right," Charles conceded. "That way."

He extended a finger in the general direction of Elm Street and Jessica felt her heart grow cold. The child had no reason to be in those streets, alone and lost. Without another word, she grabbed the hem of her fine skirt and rushed onward.

"Matty!" she yelled out, hoping her voice would carry the boy to her. "Matty, where are ye, darling?"

The day's light began to fade away and worry gripped Jessica's gut like a vice. As the last of the sun slipped behind the Thames, a bitter chill washed over her, spawning more from her apprehension than the lack of sunlight.

A soft sobbing met her ears and Jessica sprinted toward the alleyway, praying it was not another yowling feline. She stared at the small, trembling figure, crouched against the stone walls, pity consuming her soul.

"Matty!" she gasped, running toward him. He raised his head, dark eyes red from hours of crying. "What in God's good name are ye doing out here on yer own?"

He shook his head, blubbering as mucus dribbled under his nose. Jessica dug the handkerchief Father Allen had given her from her sash and wiped his tears away. She realised how close they stood to the shopfront they had once lived in and the thought sent shivers of revulsion through her.

"Where's Jake?" the little boy moaned. "Pa said—"

"Never mind what he said—and he isn't yer pa," Jessica interjected sharply. Her harsh words forced more wailing from the child. She was instantly contrite, pulling the boy to her bosom to curl on the ground beside him.

From her mouth, a hum began, her body rocking the shivering child with his holed clothes and bare feet. Slowly,

Matty relaxed in her arms and Jessica became aware that she was wordlessly singing the song from her dream.

Ensuring that the boy was calm, Jessica tapped his rear gently.

"Come along, Matty," she murmured, the cold of night seeping into her bones, the fine dress covered in soot and grime now. "Let's find ye something te eat."

Eagerly, the boy scrambled to his feet and Jessica took his hand, leading the way back to the Killinger house.

"I don't think they're there anymore," Matty mumbled. Jessica paused and gazed at the boy.

"What do ye mean?"

Matty shrugged, unable to add anymore to his suspicions but as she neared the house, sixteen furlongs from Elm Street, an uneasy silence met Jessica's ears. She swallowed her apprehension and inched her way toward the back gate, eyes scanning.

"Jessie, I don't like it 'ere," Matty complained.

"Nor do I," Jessica reassured him. "But I must find the others and take ye all te safety."

"Where?" Matty demanded, his intelligent eyes dubious. "There's nowhere te go."

It was a question that Jessica had asked herself. Anywhere away from Gareth was a start. She and the others could find their way closer to the church where they could seek out Father Thompson or Father Allen for help.

Perhaps Mrs Barlow will mind Matty a while.

"'Ello?" Jessica called bravely, tugging on Matty's arm. The boy seemed reluctant to follow.

"Ye done messed up 'is face," Matty reminded her. Jessica shuddered at the memory. She quickened her pace, realising that the house, was in fact empty. She called out again to be sure but as she scoured the area for signs of her siblings, she came across the sight that she had both anticipated and dreaded.

Jake's sack sat tucked away among Gareth's few possessions, his pocketknife and lucky penny inside.

Oh no, 'e wouldn't 'ave left these behind. His clothes too.

She ushered Matty back down the stairs, averting her eyes to the blood which remained from Gareth's attack. Had that only been a few hours ago? She felt as though it had been a lifetime.

On the main floor, near the hearth, another sight stilled Jessica's heart. Erin's only kerchief lay half in the fireplace, stained with spots of blood. Inhaling, she turned away to scour for blankets and sweaters to endure the night on the street. Every moment spent in their hideout was one closer to seeing Gareth again.

"Is there any supper, Jessie?" Matty whimpered. "My gut is on fire."

"Be patient, darling. We'll find something."

A knock at the front door caused Jessica to gasp. She yanked Matty away from the windows, her pulse roaring in her ears. Again, a gentle rap tapped at the wood.

"Hello?" The door opened and a young man entered cautiously, wrinkling his nose as he took in the disarray of the house. Jessica pushed Matty behind her, half-hiding her among her skirts.

"Come one step closer and I'll pluck out yer eyes!" Jessica called out. The stranger stopped, blinking in the darkness. His hand rose, showing fingerless gloves and filthy hands. Jessica imagined him a dock worker but she could not fathom why he was there.

Kin of the Killingers perhaps?

"I mean you no harm," he husked without venturing closer.

"What are ye doing here?"

"I've been told that Erin may reside here but I'm clearly mistaken. Forgive the intrusion."

He was well spoken for such a low-born, working boy but it was the worry in his eyes that lowered Jessica's guard.

"Who might you be?" she demanded before he could scurry off into the night. He half-turned to look at her.

"Philip Rodgers," he explained. "I...I've come to know Erin a wee bit. Do you know her?"

His hands remained up but Jessica noted the way he scoured the sorry sight of the house. The aftermath of Gareth's rages had left the once pretty place in shambles, the smell overwhelming, even to Jessica's seasoned nostrils.

We never could've 'ad a flat of our own. Gareth ruins everything he touches. 'Ow did I not see that before?

"Ye care for 'er?" Jessica challenged. "For Erin?"

The young man's eyes grew and he nodded without hesitation, fully pivoting to stare at Jessica.

"I—yes…who *are* you?"

"I'm 'er sister." Philip's face relaxed and he offered her a tentative smile.

"Jessica Joy," he announced. A fission of pleasure sparked in Jessica's chest but she did not allow herself to enjoy it.

"If ye care about 'er, really, truly love 'er, you'll see fit te take 'er and the children far from 'ere."

Philip bit down on his lip, taking Jessica's words to heart.

"She isn't safe 'ere. None of them are."

None of us are.

"I sensed as much," Philip murmured. "There's such a melancholy about her, a wisdom much older than she could ever be."

His wistful words sent pangs through Jessica's chest but they had been there long enough.

"Then ye'll do what's right, yes?"

Jessica grabbed Matty's hand and spun to leave through the back door.

"Where are you going? Do you know where I might find Erin?" Philip called out hopefully. His plaintive tone struck another chord in Jessica's hardened heart.

"No," she answered honestly. "But if ye do find her, take 'er and don't return."

She shoved Matty out of the little house, glancing in all directions to ensure she did not stumble upon Gareth.

"And what of me?" Matty squeaked, trudging after Jessica.

"What of you?" she snapped, clinging to his cold palm tightly.

"What will become of me?"

Jessica stopped in her tracks and dropped to her knees.

"I will take care of ye, just like I always 'ave," she promised.

"With Jake?"

Jessica pressed her mouth tightly together, fearsome that a cry might escape.

"Come along, now." She sighed, standing again. "We've got to get away from 'ere."

CHAPTER 12

*J*essica's hands were raw but clean, the scent of fresh soap filling her nose. Her back and legs ached from the countless hours of washing she had done but the jingle of coin in her satchel broke through all the pains of her body.

She had earned her first pay, wholesomely and honestly. The work was as gruelling and exhausting as Mrs Barlow had warned but the realisation that she had made money without sacrificing her morality put a smile upon her face that lit up the entire dockside.

Men whistled lewdly, despite her sweaty work dress.

Edward and Charles sat among their crates, cooing like pigeons as she passed.

"Hush yer mouths," she warned them, her eyes twinkling.

"We're seeing an awful lot of ye in these parts, Miss Jessie," Charles commented. "'Ave ye taken a husband?"

Jessica blushed and shook her head.

"No. A job," she informed them, pausing to stop and share a word with the begotten souls of the docks.

"Ye sure do glow for a working lady," Eddie guffawed. Jessica's beam grew. She had more than one reason to smile.

"Gareth's been up and down lookin' for ye."

Jessica's smile faded entirely.

"What?"

The brothers exchanged a drunken glance, their eyes an identical bloodshot red.

"Ye kin barely recognise 'im," Edward added, a small smirk forming on his lips. "Attacked by a fox, I 'eard."

"A falcon!" Charles insisted. "Went te peck 'is eyes out."

"Off wit ye now," Edward grumbled. "T'was a fox."

"Falcon!" Charles insisted.

"What did ye tell 'im?" Jessica demanded, waxing at the thought that Gareth had been so close without her knowledge. The brothers turned their gazes upon her, shrugging.

"Jessie who?" they chorused. A smidgen of relief twinged in her but not enough to comfort her entirely.

"But 'e did find the bairn," Edward added. "Dragged 'im off by 'is 'air not 'alf an 'our passed."

Jessica's eyes bulged.

"Marcus," Edward announced, appearing proud of his memory.

"Matty, ye daft twit," his brother snapped.

"Matty!" she choked, spinning to race off in the opposite direction. In the week since she had taken the boy away, Jessica had encountered Erin once on the street.

"I'm to marry Philip Rodgers," she confessed in a whisper, pulling her street sister into an alley. "He told me you convinced him of his love for me."

Her grey eyes shone with more happiness than Jessica had ever seen.

"I'm pleased te 'ear it," she told Erin sincerely. "But what of Drake and Anna?"

Erin had looked away guiltily.

"Pa doesn't know of my plans."

That had gone without saying to Jessica's mind.

"We'll need to sneak off in the night," she went on, eying Jessica with pleading for understanding.

"I'll return for them, once we've settled," Erin promised and Jessica had swallowed her protests. She could not do more than she was already doing for Matty and she could not fault Erin for making a better way for herself.

Mrs Barlow said it best; we cannot 'elp anyone without 'elping ourselves first.

"We've returned to Elm Street," Erin rushed on before Jessica could slip away. "So you'll know where to look for the children, should you find yourself in a position to take them too."

Jessica thought of this now as she raced through the streets, oblivious to the cries of dismay as she brushed past passersby, determined to find Matty.

The sounds of screaming met her ears before Jessica saw her small charge, holding a familiar item in his hand. Jessica paused at the end of the alleyway, gaze unsure of where to rest.

There was the flimsy coat in Matty's hands, slashed and caked with blood. Jessica's knees buckled to recognise it as Jake's.

Gareth stood menacingly over the boy, his back to her but the profile of his face showed the damage she had done in her escape from his clutches.

"Keep up your wailing," Gareth hissed. "And you'll meet the same fate as Jake."

He raised his hand to strike Matty and Jessica yelled out, her protective instinct outweighing her dizzying fear.

"Don't ye touch him!" she howled, rushing forward. Gareth whirled around, his features twisting with fury to see her.

"There you are!" he cried as if he had won a prize. Matty forgotten, he strode toward Jessica, meeting her halfway down the alley. Ruthlessly and without hesitation, he took hold of her red tresses and began to drag her.

"No! Pa, don't!" Matty screamed.

"Shut your flipping trap, boy. I'm not finished with you, either!"

Jessica kicked out, grabbing at Gareth's hands as he violently pulled her along the laneway.

"UNHAND HER AT ONCE!"

Startled, Gareth loosened his hold on Jessica and she managed to straighten herself. Amazement coloured her cheeks to see Father Allen at the far end of the tunnel, his arm raised.

St. Michael! Jessica thought as two constables appeared on either side of the clergyman.

"That's the one," Father Allen declared. "He's the kidnapper and exploiter of children."

Gareth scoffed as the policemen rushed toward him.

"I haven't the foggiest notion what he's on about," Gareth growled, his eyes darting about for means of escape. Matty threw himself into Jessica's arms and she inched them toward Father Allen.

"Father," Jessica breathed. "What is the meaning of this?"

Tenderly, Father Allen placed his hands over Jessica's shoulders, searching her face for any indication of injury.

"That man will never harm you or your family again," he promised. "I've learnt who he is, Jessica, and you were correct. Mr Winston was the same man I saw all those years ago, the man who lived by the docks and was taken in by that kindly couple."

Jessica's eyes widened.

"But the rest of the story is not so pleasant, I'm afraid."

"You bloody busybody!" Gareth spat as the bobby's shoved him along, his hands bound tightly, the pair struggling against his massive frame. Father Allen held his stare evenly, unfazed by Gareth's rantings. Realising this, Gareth whipped his head around to look at Jessica.

"You!" he snarled. "You have ruined your family! You're nothing without me!"

"Take him from our sight," Father Allen growled, turning his back to block Gareth's view of them.

"B-but…" Jessica sputtered. "He didn't kidnap us. He…" she was reluctant to use the word "save".

"Well, 'e took us in when no one else wanted us! How will the charges ever stick?"

Father Allen's face darkened. A hand reached up to touch her face.

"My poor, sweet child," he muttered. "That monster took you from a real family, one who loved you and could have provided well for you."

Stunned, Jessica blinked. She shook her head, tightening her hold against Matty's quivering body.

"No, that's not so. I was abandoned on the street, just like the others," she insisted.

"No, Jessica. You were the child of that couple, the ones I saw. Gareth Winston stole you in the night, rewarding their kindness with terror and sorrow."

Jessica gasped, falling back against a wall, her hand extended to catch herself but it was Father Allen who caught her.

"I've spent the last few weeks searching baptism records, hoping to find a trace of where you came from. There were only two Jessica's baptised between 1835 and 1837, which I guessed your year of birth to be around."

Her breath caught, anticipation creating beads of perspiration over her brow.

"One of the girls lives with her family in the North End. The other is you."

Once more, Jessica shook her head, unable to believe it.

"'Ow can ye be certain?" she pressed. Gently, Father Allen stroked her cheek, the affection in his stare tangible. Matty clung to her legs, peering out from behind her skirts to hear Father Allen's response.

"I've met with your family—what remains of it. You are undoubtedly the girl lost all those years ago."

"Y-ye've met with them?!" she gasped, trembling at the notion.

"Yes…and I will take you to meet them if you want me to."

She nodded slowly, her mind whirling with the revelations. Matty tugged on her hem again and she shook off the surreal haziness that had encompassed her.

"What of Matty?" she asked, squeezing the child's shoulders. "And Annaleigh and Drake? What of all the others?"

"I cannot speak to the other two children but young Matthew does not appear to have a legitimate birth record. I vow to continue looking but I will see Annaleigh and Drake placed in proper care with congregants of the church. I've already made the arrangements."

"Matty—" Jessica started to protest, but he stopped her.

"Will remain with us."

Jessica stared at him, uncomprehendingly.

"At the church?" she asked dumbly. She could think of worse places for the boy to be, her own memories of the warm bed and hot soup still so fresh in her mind.

"No, Jessica," Father Allen replied softly. "With you and me, should you agree to my proposal of marriage."

Stunned, she reeled back, mouth falling open. The priest chuckled.

"I cannot offer you much but a roof and a full belly but I do promise to watch over and protect you and Matty for as long as we both shall live."

Tears filled Jessica's eyes.

"Ye would marry a wretch like me?"

His eyes shadowed and again, he closed the small space between them, both hands cupping her face now.

"You are not a wretch, Jessica Joy. You are kind and resourceful. You are a mother to Matty and a girl filled with promise. I must have loved you from the first moment I saw you, laying on the ground of the cemetery but I was too foolish to realise how much until I saw you sacrifice yourself to save young Matty. It would be my honour and privilege to be at your side for the rest of our lives."

As much as Jessica blinked, she could not stop the tears from falling down her cheeks, a joy she had never known seizing her heart until she feared she might burst.

"I don't know what te say," she whispered, nodding her consent.

"Ye should say yes," Matty informed her. Father Allen laughed and embraced Jessica quickly before releasing her.

"I should not have asked you yet," he said, diminishing the growing light in Jessica's heart.

Fool! She cursed herself. *Of course 'e doesn't want the likes of me.*

"I should ask your brother for your hand first."

Jessica sighed, her eyes darting toward Jake's fallen jacket.

"I fear 'e's in no position to accept or decline," she murmured. Benevolently, he slipped a wayward strand of hair behind her ear.

"I was referring to your blood brother, Jessica," he explained softly.

"Me what?"

"You have a brother. His name is...Michael."

Jessica gasped in disbelief.

"Truly?"

Father Allen—Henry—nodded.

"Yes. And he's eager to see you after all this time. Come along. I am also eager to ask his permission for your hand."

He offered her his arm and Jessica accepted, allowing him to guide her out of the darkening alleyway, Matty at her side. She cast one last glance at the street behind her, knowing that it was the last time she would ever set eyes upon the laneway that had housed most of her youth.

Good riddance too, she thought, quickly hurrying away to leave the urchin girl she thought herself to be in her wake.

EPILOGUE

Her brother yielded the brush with awkward precision, hands separating strands as Jessica adjusted the mass of her white skirts. He had insisted on helping her with her hair, dismissing Mrs Barlow and the other congregants who had come to offer their assistance in the upcoming nuptials.

"Ye've done this before," she commented, studying his pensive expression.

"Yes," Michael replied, meeting her eyes in the mirror. "With you."

Michael's hair was as fiery red as his sister's but his eyes were a solemn brown which reminded Jessica of Matty.

Jessica turned on her stool to gawk at him.

"Ye brushed me 'air?" she asked, a now-familiar jolt of excitement tickling her gut. Every new piece of information she learned over the past months had filled her with optimism. She had not been discarded like rubbish after all.

Once, she had been well-loved and from a well-to-do family. Michael was proof of it all.

"Yes," he replied. "Mother loved to bathe you in lavender and rosewater but she would always permit me to brush and braid your hair."

"Lavender and rosewater?"

The dream flooded back in flash. Gently, Michael turned her back toward the glass and continued to stroke her tresses.

"I wish she and father were here to see this day, Jessica. They never stopped pining for you."

She caught the note of upset in his words and eyed him curiously.

"I should have done more to stop him," Michael muttered, shifting his eyes away from the mirror but his hands never slowed. Jessica reached for his palms, forcing him to look at her.

"Ye were a boy of six and I was three," she reminded him. "What could ye have done?"

Michael shrugged.

"More."

Jessica shook her head.

"No," she countered. "Ye must rid yerself of the shame."

"I feel as though I have been living with the guilt of that night every day. I want to do something to ease my conscience, Jessica."

She recognised his shame. For years, she had carried the same burden upon her own shoulders but for different reasons. Jessica studied him a moment, her pulse racing as she suddenly knew how to save them both.

"Ye owe me nothing but I may 'ave a task for ye, if ye would be so inclined."

Standing, she made her way toward the wardrobe which housed dresses more beautiful than Jessica had ever dreamt of owning. The room in which she stood had once belonged to her mother and father, Michael refusing to claim it as his own, even prior to his sister's arrival.

"What have you there?" Michael asked, wrinkling his nose as she withdrew several water-stained sheets of paper, half-formed and peeling as she spread them over the writing desk. She still could not read the copied marks on the pages but she was certain her brother could.

"This is a list of all the graves I've robbed," she admitted in a rush of breath, cheeks tinging crimson. "I copied the words as I saw them but I don't know what they say."

Michael inched toward her, reading over her shoulder.

"I would like for ye to find the families and recompense them for the troubles I've caused," she blurted out, humiliation staining her cheeks. Michael put a comforting hand on her shoulder.

"You were a child, bred to steal by a Godless man," he murmured. "None of what's come to be is your doing."

"All the same, I'd like the families made whole again."

Michael nodded.

"I will do this for you," he promised. "If you'll permit me the opportunity to finish your hair. Your betrothed will damn me to Hell if we keep him waiting much longer."

Giggling, Jessica allowed herself to be led back to the vanity.

She was getting married today to the man she had loved since she was a child. She was surrounded by family and love. Her soul was pure and happy. It was bound to be a beautiful day.

∽

Matty stood solemnly at Henry's side, clearly taking his role seriously. Yet he could not stop his face from lighting up when he rested his eyes on Jessica.

The past months had seen him well fed, the sickly pallor that had haunted him for years, vanishing under a good diet and shelter.

Michael clung to Jessica's hand as they descended the aisle, his face alight with pride.

They stopped before the pulpit, Michael lowering Jessica's hand into Henry's and the priest smiled.

Father Thompson beamed brightly but Jessica barely noticed anything but the handsome man before her. Through her peripheral vision, she saw Mrs Barlow standing proudly at her side. The door to the church opened, stealing Jessica's attention. She gasped aloud to see Erin in a simple but pretty dress, hurrying inside with Philip Rodgers on her hand. They slipped into a pew at the back of the church, casting apologetic glances about as they did. A lump formed in Jessica's throat but as she turned back to her husband-to-be, she caught sight of another two faces she had grown to love.

Drake wore a smile like she had never seen, his hair combed and face washed. Annaleigh waved wildly until her mother captured her hand and set it down, a sheepish expression touching her face. The children had found their rightful parents only two months earlier and Jessica had been afraid that she would never see them again.

"There'll be time enough to see them after we're wed," Henry promised, his voice a low whisper. Jessica swallowed the stone in her throat, her heart prepared to burst as she set her eyes back on Henry.

"You look absolutely beautiful," he told her. Jessica flushed and clung to his hands as Father Thompson cleared his throat.

"Shall we proceed?" the older priest asked. "This union has been years in the making. I suggest we not waste another moment."

"Hear hear!" Matty yelled out. The church chuckled and Jessica hushed him gently, her smile reaching each ear.

"Dearly beloved, we are gathered here today in the matter of matrimony between this man, Henry Allen, and this woman, Jessica Forrester…"

Jessica was lost in Henry's locked stare, Father Thompson's voice drifting in and out of her ears as each word erased more of her sordid past and brought her closer to Henry's arms.

She recited her vows, repeating after Father Thompson but her eyes never strayed from Henry's until the older pastor announced the words she had deigned to hear.

"By the power vested in me, by the church and God, I now pronounce you man and wife. Father Allen, you may kiss your bride."

Jessica did not permit him the chance to move, her arms flinging around his neck to draw him toward her lips, her heart pounding as their mouths touched. A light wave of laughter flowed through the church as they parted, and Henry smiled at her.

"I'll forever love and cherish you, Jessica Joy," he whispered. "Even when I am in my grave—something you know a bit about."

Jessica groaned at his joke and shook her head.

"No," she replied. "I know nothing of that life now. I only know that I am Jessica Allen, and I am your wife from this moment on..."

~*~*~

Thank you so much for reading my story.

If you enjoyed reading this book may I suggest that you might also like to read my recent release 'Saving the Wretched Slum Girl' next which is available on Amazon for just £0.99 or free with Kindle Unlimited.

Click Here to Get Your Copy Today!

Sample of First Chapter

Seven-year-old Alice Smythe was small for her age, which in some ways was a bonus as it allowed her to work as a scavenger mule at the Langford Cotton Mill, in the East End of London. She and her mother had worked there together for the past six months, Alice having commenced her employment at the mill the day after her seventh birthday.

They toiled from dawn till dusk often not seeing the outside light during the day at all. She listened intently to the clacking of the machinery as it moved back and forth, the spindle catching the yarn at the top and winding it up, as if it were a spinning top she had seen once at the travelling fair.

Alice needed to be careful when she scrambled underneath, she knew the work was dangerous—her mother had reminded her many times—but her family needed the money to survive. The loud deafening sound of the busy machinery no longer hurt her ears as it had in her first few months, her mother had told her to push some cotton fluff in them to dull the noise and she wore a remnant of cloth across her mouth to keep the loose threads and cotton dust from clogging up her throat and lungs.

Her mother suffered from a nasty cough, brought on by years of working in the hot, humid conditions that were needed in a cotton mill. She would hear her in the middle of the night getting up gasping for air, drinking to try and relieve the spasms, but nothing seemed to help. Her cough was getting much worse but still she needed to work else they would end up in the workhouse and that would be dishonourable beyond words. No one ever wanted to end up there, it would be a disgrace.

As quick as a mouse, she darted under the dangerous mechanical movement, keeping her head low, almost touching the filthy wooden floor as she gathered up the loose cotton balls that had fallen from the equipment. Her small nimble fingers tucked them into the pocket of the dark apron that her mother had placed around her waist just this morning. Dashing forward before the machine could complete another turn, Alice darted out on the other side—she was safe this time.

Even at the young age of seven, Alice knew that there was a heavy risk around the machines. Her mother would warn her several times a day to be careful about watching her head and keeping her wits about her at all times. While she didn't enjoy the task she had been given, Alice knew that her family badly needed the extra money now that her father wasn't able to work. It was up to Alice and her mother, Mary to find the necessary finances to support them. They were luckier than some, she was an only child, Alice couldn't imagine how hard it must be for families with several children.

Alice hurried around the machine, placing the loose cotton scraps into the storage barrel that would be taken away at the end of the day, dumping the oddments into the large vats of leftover fragments. Alice liked the way the soft cotton felt between her fingertips. Just the other day she had put some in her pocket and taken it home, keeping it under her pillow to touch in the cold dark nights. She would have been whipped by Master Turney, the foreman, if he had found out, but Alice hadn't been forced to empty her pockets that particular day, so no one knew and now she had something of her own that no one else knew about.

Not even her mother…

"Alice! Stop daydreaming. The cotton isn't going to pick itself up!"

Her mother's voice cut through her thoughts and Alice darted under the machine once more, gathering up the cotton. A few strands of fine blonde hair clung to Alice's moist neck as she quickly finished her task. Her mother made her wear a dark brown mop cap so that her hair wouldn't get trapped in the constantly moving machinery above her head, telling her daughter that she had seen it happen once, that a little girl had been scalped before they could stop the machines. All of Alice's clothes were either brown or black in colour, her mother insisted that she wear dark clothing. After all, you couldn't see the dirt if it was the same colour as the material, she would say.

"Smythe!"

Alice cringed at the sound of Master Turney's shrill voice, scurrying out of his path as he bared down on her mother. Having worked at the Langford Cotton Mill for most of her life, her mother didn't even flinch at the man's putrid breath hovering over her. "Yes, Master Turney?" she answered plainly.

He pointed at Alice, who was peeking out from behind one of the machines. "Why isn't your gel sweeping the floor like she is paid to do?" the man growled angrily.

"I will have her do it straightaway, Master Turney," her mother replied. Alice didn't waste any time finding the broom. Hurrying as far away as possible from the conversation, she set to sweeping up the dust and cotton fragments too small to be picked up. She didn't like Master Turney and very few workers at the factory did. He was a nasty vicious bully, who wouldn't think twice about using his fists to get what he wanted.

Her small body moved the broom furiously over the grimy floor, causing a small cloud of dust to rise which tickled her nose through her face covering, but she managed not to sneeze. In the near distance, she saw a familiar face, nine-year-old John Cartwright, walking through the hallway. It was unbelievable that he was back at work so soon after his terrible accident.

He was one of the piecers, a job known to be very dangerous, and John had proved the point. He had not been in work for the past few days. Alice remembered back to the day when John had been hurt, she had never seen so much blood before in her young life and, despite the fact that her mother had tried to shield her from it, Alice had still seen enough of the carnage to scare her for a lifetime.

Poor John had got his hand caught trying to repair the broken threads, he had foolishly tried to grab his cap that had been dislodged because he was growing too tall.

"What's he doin' here, he canna work like that?" the foreman shouted above the roar of the machines. "Look at that bandage, there's still blood seeping through."

"I promise ye he can still work, just as well. He's a strong lad. Put him on moving the barrels or helping with sweeping the floors. Please, I beg of ye," his mother, Myrtle pleaded. She was a thin scraggy woman and most folks in the factory knew that John and Myrtle depended on the work to support his younger siblings. His father had passed just five months ago from the same cough that Alice's poor mother was displaying.

Alice swallowed as her eyes trailed towards the bandage, gasping when she realised that it was evident that two of his fingers were not where they should be.

Shaking his head, Turney relented, sending John to the docking area where the cotton came in to be sent to the looms, yelling for the trembling woman to get back to her work too. The rest of the day passed by slowly and without incident and by the time the sun was starting to fade through the filth ingrained windows, Alice's hands were covered in fresh bulging blisters from holding the broom far too tightly.

Passing down the last aisle, she swept the dust away from the pathways between the looms. Just as she was finishing up, she heard raised voices and crept a little closer to the sound.

"I don't care what you were doing! You weren't here, Nicholas! That is all that matters. I want you here and in *my* bed at night."

"Now, you listen to me, I had business to attend to, Catherine. You couldn't possibly understand what I was doing."

Alice took a quick peek in the direction the voices were coming from, her eyes widening, when she saw the owner of the Mill, Mr Nicholas Langford, standing close by, next to his wife, Catherine Langford. Mr Langford was dressed in a fine dark charcoal grey suit, the shiny golden chain of a pocket watch swaying across the front of his rather portly stomach that was covered by colourful floral waistcoat. Catherine Langford was dressed in a gown that was perhaps the loveliest that Alice had ever seen, having a deep crimson colour with pretty cream coloured lacework at the neck and cuffs. Alice wondered if the material felt as soft and smooth as it looked.

She would never attempt to touch the fabric, however, that would never do, it would be cause for instant dismissal. She could see that Catherine Langford was annoyed as she glared angrily at her husband. Alice had seen that stance many times before. It was the same one that her mother liked to use when Alice was misbehaving. She was intrigued to know what was going on and she couldn't help but stand stock still and gawp as the couple continued to argue.

"Oh, Nicholas, I'm well aware of what you were doing," Catherine Langford said, her hands flying about wildly. "You were with that hussy again, weren't you?"

Mr Langford stepped forward, hands raised as he tried to placate his angry wife. "Come, come, you don't know what you are talking about."

Catherine Langford laughed audibly and there was a bitterness to the high-pitched sound. "Oh, Nicholas, I am not as naïve as you may think. I know you have a mistress and have done for some time." Alice gasped at the woman's strange words. She knew she shouldn't continue to listen to another's private conversation, but she simply couldn't help herself. Catherine Langford continued speaking, her voice a little lower now. "That is not why I sought you out though. Our son, Matthew, is due to return from school for the summer break. I expect he will be going back at the start of the autumn term."

"Mm-hm," Nicholas acknowledged, clearing his throat. "I'm not sure that is a good idea. I suggest he comes to work in the mill so he can come to understand some of what he is destined to inherit. It's about time he learnt the family trade. That's how I learnt the goings on of this establishment—from my father, not by spending money on an expensive education."

"I understand, but he will still be returning to school to finish his education. I insist," Mrs Langford stated plainly, pushing her index finger into the man's chest to prove her point. "He's destined for greatness. He may not have a title, but that does not matter in this time of vast economic growth."

"As you well know, my darling," the man replied, a cruel sneer spreading across his face. "This is our livelihood. It is what pays for your fancy gowns and afternoon teas with those simpering women you call your friends. Of course, he will finish the necessary education but then he is expected to learn how to run this factory. Too much of a fancy education isn't going to help without the practical experience to help him get on in life."

Catherine Langford didn't look as if she was about to back down and Alice waited to see what the man would do next. "As long as you allow him to complete his studies, I will be satisfied," she said placing her hands firmly on her hips. "But you are not to renege on your word."

"S'cuse me, Mr Langford. We need to talk about them workers and which ones ain't pulling their weight and what we need to do about 'em?"

The couple turned as Master Turney approached them, causing Alice to shrink back into the shadows, her young mind attempting to sort out the conversation she had just overheard. So, the owner had a son, one that she was not aware of. What good fortune he had, never needing to work in this grimy, dirt-laden mill but going to school to learn to read and write, something she had always dreamt of doing.

Sighing with frustration, she quickly finished her work before making her way back to her mother. "Ready, my darling gel?" her mother asked trying to smother a cough, tightening the scarf around her head and handing Alice her coat. "There is a cold wind out there. We wouldn't want to catch our deaths, so button up and come along with me," she continued holding out her hand for Alice to take.

Alice donned her coat and thin woollen scarf before making their way down the stone steps with the other workers, their workday finally at an end. Alice stayed close to her mother as they exited the mill, grasping her hand lightly. The lamp lighters were already out, lighting the smoggy streets, allowing them a dull glow with which to find their way home. By the time they got back, Alice's nose was red and streaming from the cold.

Her father eagerly awaited them inside, leaning heavily on his crutch as they entered in a flurry. "There you are," he cried as Alice shrugged out of her coat. "I have made us some dinner."

Her mother gave him a grateful smile, knowing that there was little food to be had and it would have been difficult to cook something nourishing for them all. "That was kind of you, Frank. I'm sorry we are late."

Alice gave her father a tight hug, careful not to topple him over. "Thank you, Papa."

"Oh, my darling gel. You don't have to thank me for anything," he said, returning her embrace.

Alice gazed up at him and saw the sadness in his eyes as he looked down at her. Her father had also once worked in the mill. However, an inexperienced hand had incorrectly stacked some barrels, causing them to escape their confines, crushing his leg beyond repair. With his badly deformed leg and the crutch he required to get around, no mill was willing to offer him work—to them he was as good as useless.

It didn't matter to Alice, though, he was still her Papa and she loved him more than anybody else in the world, apart from her Mama of course, who she loved equally.

"Come, Alice," her mother said pulling her towards the enamel washbasin. "Let's get cleaned up."

Alice dutifully did as her mother asked, forcing her hands into the frigid water.

Her stomach grumbled, reminding her of how hungry she was, although there would be barely enough food, being that the family had to survive on the pittance that she and her mother earned. Times may be hard in the Smythe household, but Alice knew there was always plenty of love to go around.

~*~*~

This wonderful Victorian Romance story — 'Saving the Wretched Slum Girl' — is available on Amazon for just £0.99 or *FREE* with Kindle Unlimited simply by clicking on the link below.

[Click Here to Get Your Copy of 'Saving the Wretched Slum Girl' - Today!](#)

A NOTE FROM THE AUTHOR

Dear Reader,

Thank you so much for choosing and reading my story — I sincerely hope it lived up to your expectations and that you enjoyed it as much as I loved writing about the Victorian era.

This age was a time of great industrial expansion with new inventions and advancements.

However, it is true to say that there was a distinct disparity amongst the population at that time — one that I like to emphasise, allowing the characters in my stories to have the chance to grow and change their lives for the better.

Best Wishes
Ella Cornish

∽

Newsletter

If you love reading Victorian Romance stories…

Simply sign up here and get your FREE copy of The Orphan's Despair

Click Here to Download Your Copy - Today!

∼

More Stories from Ella!

If you enjoyed reading this story you can find more great reads from Ella on Amazon…

Click Here for More Stories from Ella Cornish

∼

Contact Me

If you'd simply like to drop us a line you can contact us at **ellacornishauthor@gmail.com**

You can also connect with me on my Facebook Page **https://www.facebook.com/ellacornishauthor/**

I will always let you know about new releases on my Facebook page, so it is worth liking that if you get the chance.

LIKE Ella's Facebook Page *__HERE__*

I welcome your thoughts and would love to hear from you!

Printed in Great Britain
by Amazon